CUT LOOSE

A Hellhounds MC romance

Stacey Broadbent

Published by Stacey Broadbent, Ashburton, NZ
Copyright 2021 © Stacey Broadbent

Originally part of the HellHounds Anthology
This is the extended version.

Proofreading by Spell Bound
Cover image from Deposit Photos
Cover Design by Stacey Broadbent

ISBN: 978-0-473-63651-7 (paperback)
        978-0-473-63652-4 (Kindle)

CUT LOOSE

A Hellhounds MC romance

Stacey Broadbent

AUTHOR'S NOTE

The characters in this story are from New Zealand, therefore UK spelling and terms have been used. Please remember these are not errors, it's just the way we do things here.

***Please also note* this story contains scenes of a graphic nature and may contain triggers, involving domestic abuse, abduction, and drug use.**

PROLOGUE

SAM

The trouble with small towns is that everyone thinks they're entitled to know your business. I am a private person. I don't like my dirty washing being aired out for all to see. I'd hoped for a little anonymity when I chose to leave, and now on my fifth town in as many months, I'm tired of running. All I wanted was to pack up the few things that mattered to me and start afresh. To slip in quietly, settle into my new home, and keep to myself. Is that so much to ask?

I don't want people sticking their noses in where they're not wanted. That's one of the reasons I left; no privacy. I could barely sneeze without someone knowing about it. Chaperoned by men in dark suits and glasses everywhere I went, having to ask permission to go to the damn bathroom, never having a minute of solitude; it takes its toll. I've spent the last five years pretending to the outside world that life was a dream, while on the inside I was slowly dying.

Breaking free was my only saving grace. To hell with the consequences. I lived for the moment I could stand on my own two feet with no one shadowing my every move. To be able to stand on the beach and dig my toes in the sand without an army surrounding me. To finally be able to breathe again.

But breathing doesn't come cheap, and as much as I want to hide away in my little beach house by the ocean, I need money to survive. The small amount I'd managed to get away with is dwindling, and I'll be lucky if it will last more than a few weeks without a cash injection. I have nothing of value. Nothing to sell for a quick buck. That means I need to find a job. With people. The very thing I've been trying to avoid. But like I said, people in small towns always want to know every sordid detail of your life. Details I'd rather remain hidden, for my safety and theirs.

I haven't had a job since I was fresh out of high school, and even then, it was short-lived. Dante refused to let me work, saying it was beneath me, but really it was just another way to control me. To keep me under his thumb.

But this is what I fought for; a life of my own, and that means I have to pull up my big-girl panties and get on with it. Let them talk all they want; it doesn't mean I have to let them in. It doesn't mean I have to share my story. It means I get to make a new story.

CHAPTER ONE

SAM

"Hi, welcome to A Cut Above, have you got an appointment?" The redhead at reception looks up from her nail file and smiles. "Oh hey, I know you, you're that new girl renting Mr Garrison's place down on the beach, right?"

"Uh, yeah." So much for keeping to myself. I offer my hand, juggling my bag onto my shoulder. "I'm Sam Traynor. I saw your help wanted sign out front."

She cranes her neck as if reading the poster from her perch. "Oh, that position is more like for a school kid or something. Ya know? Just sweeping and cleaning up really."

"I don't mind that."

"Really? I mean, pretty face like yours should be out there selling something, ya know? Not cleanin' up after people. Plus…" She leans in, speaking in a hushed tone behind her hand, "it's not exactly paying big bucks." She waves her hand out behind her. "Business ain't exactly booming."

"That's okay. I'd rather be doing something in the background anyway. A job's a job, right?" I shrug, trying to think of something normal to say. "Gotta pay the bills."

"Ain't that the truth?" She rolls her eyes then grins. "You know what? I didn't really want a teenybopper hanging around anyways, and you don't *seem* like a serial killer. I like you. When can you start?"

Pointing to the pile of hair behind her, I quirk my brow. "I'm free now, if you like?"

She nods, pushing up from her seat. "Sure thing, chicken wing. Come out back. You can leave your bag there, and I'll show you around some." She totters off on her stiletto heels, stopping to check the foils on a client's head. "Just another couple minutes, Suzanne. I'll be right back with ya, okay?"

The woman glances up at the mirror, her eyes flicking towards me and back again before she offers a smile. "Take your time, Jen." She holds up her glossy gossip magazine. "I've got my royals to keep me company."

Jen clucks her tongue then waves me forward. Sweeping aside the saloon-style doors, she waves her arm out. "This is the staff area. You can put your bag in that cubby over there if you like." She points to a small empty cube along the wall beside the bench. "Tea and coffee are up here if you do instant, but between you and me, the coffee house on the corner is your best bet for a good cuppa java." She screws her nose up. "There's something up with the water filter in here. Always tastes like feet."

I shove my bag into the cubby, stifling a laugh. This woman doesn't appear to have any filter, and with the amount she talks, I don't see her asking too many questions, which suits me just fine.

"Over here is the utility closet. You'll find all the brooms, buckets and mops, any cleaning supplies you need, and there's a sink in here too. I try to keep it all separate from the kitchen even though I barely use it because, ya know, feet water." She shakes her head, chuckling. "We have parking spaces out back if you drive, which I assume you do living out at the beach. Long way to walk otherwise. Anyway, just look for the ones labelled A Cut Above. I like to keep the front clear for our clients. Some can get mighty titchy if they have to walk farther than a few feet to get to their appointment." She rolls her eyes, placing her hands on her hips. "That's about it, really. Any questions?"

Taking another quick glance around the room, I shake my head. "No, I think I've got it all. Don't drink the water, park out back, and the cupboard is for cleaning."

"Spot on, chickadee. Well, there's an apron over there you can use. If you wanna start with the sweeping out there, that'd be fab. I've gotta go and tend to

Suzanne's foils, and then I'll show you how to work the till."

With a nod of my head, I grab the broom and follow her out front.

"Right, let's take a look at this colour, shall we?" Jen lifts an edge of foil and hums before checking another. "Mmhmm, I think that'll do nicely, love. Come over here and we'll get it all washed out for you." She leads her to the basins at the back of the salon, throwing a wink my way as I sweep Suzanne's hair into a pile.

There's a sound like thunder rumbling, then the door chimes and a busty brunette bursts through, chewing gum loudly. The glass in the shop front vibrates as the rumbling intensifies as a gang of motorcycles roar past. The brunette skirts past the counter and straight out the back where she seems to be throwing things about. "That's Barb," Jen explains with a nod of her head. "She's having man troubles, aren't you, chicken?"

Barb pushes back through to the salon, her hands behind her back as she ties her apron. "Don't even get me started." She rolls her eyes. "Matiu is… ugh!" She throws her hands in the air as she stomps over to the basin, taking over from Jen.

"Matiu's one of the Hellhounds, and he likes to stir her up something chronic, doesn't he, love?" Jen folds her arms, her bracelets jangling. "What's he done this time?"

"What *hasn't* he done?" She flicks her hair behind her as she pumps conditioner into her hand.

I clear my throat. "I don't mean to sound rude, but what's a Hellhound?"

"Oh, silly me, of course you don't know, you're new in town." Jen chuckles, wrapping an arm around my shoulders. "The Hellhounds are the local motorcycle gang—"

"Club, not gang." Barb narrows her eyes. "We've been over this."

Jen waves a dismissive hand through the air. "Yeah, yeah. Po-tay-toe, po-tah-toe."

"A gang? Here? In Brookhaven?" To say I'm surprised is an understatement. Brookhaven has a thriving retirement community and not much else. I've never seen so many purple rinses in one place. It's certainly not the kind of town I'd expect to find a gang.

"We're not some rinky-dink town, you know? We *do* have lives here too." Barb finishes rinsing Suzanne's hair and sits her up, wrapping a towel around her head. "Who're you anyway?"

"Oh, ah, I'm Sam." I slide my hand down the side of my pants then hold it out to her. She glares at it as if offended. Dropping my hand to my side, I fidget with the hem of my top. "I, ah, work here now." I glance at Jen who smiles then turns to Barb with a stern look.

"She's our new part-timer, so be nice."

Barb holds her hands up, palms out as she raises her brows. "Alright, alright. I won't bite, I promise."

Something tells me Barb and I won't be friends anytime soon.

CHAPTER TWO

JERICHO

Pulling in round the back of Lawson's Lugs, I park the bike and lift the helmet from my head as I wait for Matiu. Things had looked a little tense there with Barb, and I didn't want to stick around and make it awkward. The stupid prick has no clue how good he's got it with her. Finding a woman who's okay with our lifestyle is nothing short of a miracle. Barb has seen her fair share of shit and for some reason she's stuck with him anyway.

I hear him before I see him. The extra kick of gas as he rounds the corner then slows to meet the drive.

Matiu pulls up beside me, killing the engine before he sets it on the stand and gives me a shit-eating grin.

"I don't know what you're so happy about, bro." I shake my head, stalking towards the garage as he falls into step beside me. "You do understand what it means to have an old lady, right? You can't just string her along like that. One of these days, Barb's gonna wake up to your shit and she's gonna leave your sorry arse."

"This coming from the guy who hasn't been laid, let alone had an old lady, in fucking years." Matiu barks out a laugh, slapping me on the back. "Thanks for the dating advice, but I think I'm good."

"I'm serious, man. If you're not careful, you're gonna lose her."

"Haven't you heard the saying, treat 'em mean, keep 'em keen before?"

I stop walking, turning my head away as I suck in a breath and remind myself he's my friend. "That's a shitty way of looking at it, and you know it."

He holds both hands up placatingly. "I'm just playin', you know that. I might act like a dick sometimes, but I'd never do nothing to hurt her."

I huff out a sigh. He's right. I know he wouldn't, but it doesn't change the fact he's skating on thin ice. "Good. I don't really wanna have to kick your arse if you do."

"Pssh, you wish, old man." He darts away, jogging over to continue the job he was doing. A 1957 Chevy Impala in pristine condition. You don't see a lot of those around here, but Aldrin, from the classic car club, struck up a deal with a guy in Christchurch, and he brought it straight here to us for a tune up. She's a beauty, and once Matiu is done with her, she should be purring like a pussy cat.

I make my way through to the office, dumping my jacket on the edge of my desk. There's a pile of mail to go through, but I push that aside, instead turning to the computer and firing it up.

While I wait for it to start, I make my way through to the staff room and make myself a coffee. Leaning my hip against the counter, I stare into the mess of my office. It's getting out of control, but filing has never been a strong point of mine. In fact, administration of any sort was never on my radar when I would come in here as a youngster and watch my dad and grandfather work under the hood of so many cars. It was always on the cards for me to take over the family business and the MC when the time was right, but it never occurred to me just how much office work was involved. Then again, he'd had Mum to help him with all that, and well, as Matiu so kindly pointed out, I don't have an old lady of my own. No one to warm my bed at night or keep me honest. No one to share the burdens or celebrate the wins.

Scrubbing a hand down my face, I grab my coffee and traipse back through to my desk. The dusty computer screen prompts me to enter my password, which I do, and the picture of a dark-haired man with a handlebar moustache leaning on a Harley Davidson comes to life. The tell-tale skull and cross bones adorning the chassis brings a smile to my face. My grandfather was my idol, and I'd spent many weekends helping him buff the chrome until it shone enough to see my reflection. He took me on my first bike ride, teaching me how to lean into the turns. Bought me my first leathers and created a bike track in his backyard for me to practise on. If it wasn't for him, there'd be no Hellhounds, and there'd be no Lawson's Lugs either. Hell, I don't even think I'd be here still if it wasn't for him giving me a reprieve and taking me away from it all.

Benedict Lawson taught me everything I needed to know about cars and becoming a man, and not a day goes by I don't think of the old guy.

A knock on the door draws my attention, and Zeb pokes his head in. The kid came to us for an apprenticeship a few months back. He's still wet behind the ears, but he's eager to prove himself, and I like that.

"What is it, kid?"

"Uh, Matiu said to tell you Holden is coming back?" He lifts his cap, scratching at his dirty-blond hair.

"That so?" I lean back in my seat, a grin spreading across my face. So he's finally coming home. Well I'll be damned. I honestly thought we wouldn't see him grace these doors again. "He say when?"

"A few weeks, I think." He sniffs, shifting from foot to foot.

"Anything else?"

"He said he was taking my place?"

Of course he did. Smart prick.

I chuckle. The kid's eager, but he's got a lot to learn if he wants to stick it out. Number one rule is to take everything Matiu says with a grain of salt. The guy is full of shit, and he loves anyone gullible enough to believe him.

"Haven't I told you not to believe everything he says? He's fucking with you, Zeb."

He huffs out a laugh. "Oh… yeah… of course. I knew that." He laughs again. "So, I can stay?"

I take a sip of my coffee and frown. "Tell you what, you go get me a decent coffee, and you can stay as long as you like."

CHAPTER THREE

SAM

The rest of the week flies by, and I have to admit, it hasn't been all that bad working at the salon. The few hours I'm doing each day is enough to wile away the time, and I've met some interesting characters. Certainly beats sitting at the beach house all by myself. There's only so much soul searching one can do, I suppose, and I've had plenty of practice over the years.

Thursday morning rolls around, and Jen has me in for the whole day. It's pension day, and that means all the old ducks in town are in for their weekly rinse and blow wave. I've never been so rushed off my feet before, but damn if it doesn't set my spirits soaring. I'd forgotten what it felt like to be busy. And, more to the point, to feel needed. Like *actually* needed and not just as a pretty thing to be seen and not heard. It is, without a doubt, one of the best days of my life. And that says a lot.

"You did good today, chickadee." Jen flips the sign on the door to closed. "Thursdays are always a little crazy here."

Barb snorts. "That's an understatement."

"Anyway, thanks for coming in for the day. We can always use an extra hand on Thursdays."

"It was my pleasure. I really enjoyed it." I grin, pushing my way through the saloon doors to retrieve my bag from out back. "Some of their stories put me to shame."

"Don't I know it?" Jen chuckles, flicking off the lights. "Retirement villages are where it's at when you get old and grey. All those little blue pills floating about."

Barb screws her nose up. "Eww, that's gross. My granny is in one of those up in Christchurch. I do *not* want that mental image of her, thank you very much." She shudders.

"Age is just a number, Barb. If you can still get it when you're 80, I say go for it." Jen holds her hand up for a high five, and I oblige. I can absolutely see her living her best life, long into her retirement.

Barb rolls her eyes. "Don't encourage her." She slings her bag onto her shoulder and pushes through to the carpark out back, a cigarette already between two fingers. With a flick of her wrist, she lights it up and takes a drag, tipping her head back and closing her eyes. "You know, you two need to get better lives outside of this place instead of living vicariously through the old folks. It's sad."

"Spoken like a true youngster with nothing but time on her hands. Not like us who have to pay bills, am I right?" Jen turns to me with a twinkle in her eye. "Though she is right. *You're* still young enough to be out there sowing your wild oats."

Barb shakes her head, and I can't help but laugh. "I'm pretty sure I don't have oats to sow, Jen."

She waves a dismissive hand. "You know what I mean. You should be going out on the town or whatever it is you young folk do for fun. Say…" She turns to Barb. "Why don't you take her out this weekend?"

"Oh, that's not necessary. I'm more of a homebody." And this time it's by choice. "I'm sure she doesn't want me hanging around."

Barb stares at me as smoke swirls out of her nose.

"Don't be silly. Barb knows all the best places to go, I'm sure. You could show her around, right, love?" Jen nods, and I'm reminded of the time my mother stepped in and found me some friends to hang out with on the first day of intermediate in a new town. I'd never been more mortified and grateful at the same time. What I wouldn't give to have her with me right now.

"Really, it's fine. I've got this book I'm reading…" I let my voice trail off as the sound of rolling engines rumbles through the evening air. Barb takes one last drag of her cigarette before dropping it to the ground and stepping on the stub.

The engines grow louder as they roar down the side street and into the carpark. Two large motorcycles with long chrome handlebars that I've often thought would be hard to steer pull up beside us. With a glance over her shoulder, Barb steps up to the one closest and waits for him to remove his helmet before draping herself across him. There's a tā moko weaving from his nose and mouth down his neck and disappearing under his leather jacket, and his knuckles are tattooed with words I can't make out. He's an imposing figure, but his eyes shine when they look at Barb, and a pang of jealousy hits me right in the chest. I wonder what that feels like, to have someone look at you the way he's looking at her. It's intimate but also possessive, and I almost feel as though I shouldn't be watching.

When I turn my gaze to the other one, I find deep brown eyes appraising me. His gaze travels up and down my body before settling on my mouth. With a smirk, he nods. "Ladies."

I raise my hand in a tiny wave and then regret it. He drags his tongue across his bottom lip, his smirk growing broader.

"Barb?" Jen nods her head toward me, then points from her hip as if she thinks no one else can see what she's doing. I know she means well, but it doesn't make it any less embarrassing.

Barb sighs, rolling her eyes. She flings her arm out to gesture between the two men. "This is Matiu, my boyfriend." She wraps a possessive hand around his bicep. "And that's Jericho Lawson, VP of the Hellhounds."

Jen grabs my arm and pulls me forward. "This here is Sam Traynor. She's new in town."

"Is that right?" Jericho raises a brow. "Where're you from, princess?"

"Oh, um, a small town up north. You probably don't know it." *Why the hell did I say that?*

"You'd be surprised what I know." His dark eyes search mine, and I hold my breath, waiting for him to ask for an answer I don't have, but he doesn't. He turns to Matiu instead. "You good?"

Matiu nods, handing Barb a helmet. She flicks her hair back and places it on her head before throwing her leg over the back of the bike to settle in behind him. Her arms wrap around his waist, not quite meeting in the middle. He twists the key, and the engine purrs beneath him. Barb wriggles in closer and grips his jacket between her fingers.

With a nod of his head, Jericho kicks off and the bike coasts slowly out of the carpark and back down the side street. And I'm left wondering why I can still feel the weight of his stare searing my skin.

CHAPTER FOUR

JERICHO

I down another whiskey, trying and failing to keep my mind on what Tony is saying and not on the haunting eyes of Sam Traynor. Eyes that have seen their fair share of pain. I'd recognise that look anywhere.

It's not your problem, Jericho. You can't save everyone.

But maybe I could save *her*. No one comes to Brookhaven of their own free will. You're either born here, or you have no other options. And Sam Traynor definitely wasn't born here.

She does look like the type to have options though. Long flowing blonde hair, the stature of a dancer, and those eyes of icy blue. She definitely looks like someone who has a nice little nest egg tucked away somewhere, a rich daddy to throw money at her problems and make them go away... or perhaps that's just it; she's exhausted her options and running is all that's left.

You're getting ahead of yourself. You don't even know her.

But I *do* know that look in her eyes. I know fear when I see it, and Sam sure as shit is scared of something.

"Jericho?" Tony clicks his fingers in front of my face, and I lurch backwards.

"What the fuck?"

"Where's your mind at, boy? You got somewhere else you need to be?"

Matiu smirks beside me, as if it wasn't him in my shoes last week.

"Sorry, Tony. What'd you say?"

"I said, is there any word on the P lab location?"

Fucking P. Whoever the sick fuck was that cooked that shit up should be shot, if they're not dead already. It's ruined so many lives, and this is the second lab that's sprung up in Brookhaven in the past few months. I'm sick of it.

"I'm working on it. I'm having Zeb do a bit of recon. Should know more tomorrow."

"We need to get on top of this shit. Another kid took his life last night." Tony shakes his head. "High off his nut, swung a rope around the rafters. His baby sister found him." He clasps his hands on the table, ducking his head. "I don't need to tell you what that does to a child."

No, he doesn't.

The memory of my sister's lifeless body swinging gently in the breeze as she hung from a tree out back is seared in my brain forever more.

His eyes meet mine before I turn away, finding a spot on the wall to stare at. I bite the inside of my cheek, my brow furrowing as I focus on breathing.

In and out.

In and out.

It wasn't your fault.

In and out.

In and out.

"Let's call it a day." Tony cracks his gavel on the table and pushes up from his seat. His hand falls onto my shoulder, giving a squeeze, and I slap my hand over his. "You good?"

I squint up at him, giving a nod. He knows better than anyone how I'm feeling right now.

Another kid lost to the mind-numbing, soul-destroying shit that is P. Another parent having to bury their child. Another child having to live with the vision of their brother hanging, engrained on their brain for the rest of their life.

P doesn't just destroy the life of the user, it decimates the lives of their loved ones too. The ones who tried to keep them clean and make them see sense when all they wanted was to escape into their darkness. The ones left behind to pick up the pieces.

Shoving my seat backwards, I push up from the table and head out to the bar with Matiu. Barb is perched on a stool at one of the tables in the centre, waiting for our business dealings to be done. The woman has the patience of a saint. I don't know what she sees in the ugly lug beside me, or why she bothers to stick around a bunch of grease monkeys, but I'm glad for it all the same. She's good for him, even if he can't see it for himself. One of these days he'll realise, I only hope it's not too late when he does.

"That didn't take long," she says as we join her. "I've only had one drink." She raises her near-empty glass to her lips and downs it in one. Grabbing the cigarette pack off the table, she taps it a few times then pulls one free, tucking it between her lips.

"Must be time for another then." Matiu plants a wet kiss to her cheek then saunters to the bar, grabbing two bottles of beer and another cider.

Barb lights her smoke then wipes a hand across her cheek with a look of amusement, and I can't help but wonder what it's like to be that taken by someone you'd welcome their sloppy kisses.

Slamming a bottle down in front of me, Matiu takes up the seat beside Barb, slinging his arm around her shoulder. He throws a smirk my way before turning to her. "So, what's Sam's deal?"

Barb quirks her brow, her lips pulling into a soft pout. "How the hell should I know?"

"Uh, you work with her." Matiu grins, tipping his head towards me. "And Jericho could do with getting laid."

I flip him the bird as I toss my drink back.

Barb snorts, stirring her finger around in her glass. "Good luck with that."

Matiu shivers, rubbing his hand up and down her arm. "Did it just get cold in here?"

"Ha-ha." Barb rolls her eyes. "But I'm not the frosty one, she is. I doubt she'd even know what to do with a man like Jericho." She winks, the corner of her mouth pulling up. "She's a homebody, said so herself. She'd rather read a book than go out." She opens her eyes wide. "Weirdo, right?"

"Aw shit, so she's smart then. No good for you, old man." Matiu cracks up laughing as he pulls a cigarette from Barb's pack. He holds it towards me, but I wave it off. No matter how many times I tell him I gave up ten years ago, he still feels the need to offer. Every. Damn. Time.

"Just because you're illiterate doesn't mean I am. I read."

"Ha! When's the last time you read anything other than a car manual?" He takes a drag from his cigarette, blowing the smoke towards me with a smirk. "And porn don't count, either."

"It does if you read the articles." I waggle my brows. "Isn't that why everyone reads porn?"

Barb snorts out a laugh. "If that's the case, Matiu's a bloody scholar, right, babe?"

"Fucking A I am." He puffs out his chest and dusts off his shoulders.

"Great, you can help me out in the office until Holden comes back."

"Yeah, nah, I don't think so, boss. Gotta use my smarts for other things, eh? The cars won't fix themselves, and your old-man hands ain't what they used to be."

"These old-man hands can still beat your arse." I flex my fingers, cracking the knuckles. "Want me to show you?"

Matiu holds up his palms. "Wouldn't want you to hurt yourself."

I shake my head, chuckling. "Jesus Christ, mate, I'm five years older than you, not a fucking geriatric. I could take you on with my eyes closed and one hand tied behind my back, and I'd still win."

"I'd pay to see that." Barb sips her drink, watching on with interest.

"Ohh, you're gonna do me like that, babe?" Matiu lets out a low whistle. "That's cold."

"Maybe, but you'd have me to nurse you better." She shrugs, and Matiu cocks his head, nodding.

"I like the sound of that."

"Already planning on losing? You do know how a fight works, right?"

"Pssh. You misunderstand me, *old man*. I'd *have* to lose, because you ain't got no one to nurse you better. I couldn't do that to you, bro." He smirks, snuffing his cigarette out in the ashtray. "I respect you too much."

I laugh, pointing a finger at his chest. "Chicken shit, and a fucking liar." I nod towards his empty bottle. "Another?"

"You know it."

CHAPTER FIVE

SAM

I wake to the soothing sound of the waves crashing against the shore, the salty scent permeating the air. The flimsy mesh fabric parading as a curtain wafts in the early morning breeze blowing gently through the open window.

Open window?

I bolt up, and a sudden wave of dizziness overwhelms me. I clutch a hand to my chest. I could've sworn I closed that before bed last night.

With my heart thundering in my chest, I roll onto my back, my eyes dancing around the room. Nothing but bare walls and my clothes folded on the chair in the corner. Exactly as I left it. I let out a shaky breath and bring a hand to rub at my forehead. He doesn't know I'm here. I left no traces behind me, I made sure of that. I'm just being paranoid.

Dragging the sheets from my body, I slide my legs over the edge and place my feet on the hardwood floor. I push up to standing and make my way over to the window, peering out before pulling it closed. Goosebumps form on my arms, and I'm not sure whether it's from the brisk air through the cracks around the edge of the window, or something more sinister.

I pull my bath robe from the back of the door and throw it over my shoulders as I pad down the hall, looking into each doorway as I go. Nothing seems out of place, and by the time I reach the kitchen, I feel as though I can breathe freely again. My mind must be playing tricks on me, making me think I closed the window last night when, in fact, I hadn't.

Flicking the switch on the jug, I head through to the bathroom to freshen up. I splash water on my face. Even with a full night's sleep, there are still bags under my eyes, and my hair colour could do with a touch up. Good thing I know the boss at A Cut Above.

I finish up in the bathroom then pour myself a strong coffee and head out to the porch. Wind whips my robe around my legs as I lean a hip against the railing and look out over the ocean. Fluffy grey clouds loom in the distance, but for now, the sky is bright with the early morning rays of sunshine. I tilt my head backwards to soak it in, inhaling deeply. It's been far too long since I've been able to 'stop and smell the roses' so to speak. Sure, I'd had everything a girl could want, and I'd lived a life of luxury, but material things only go so far. They don't compare to the life of love that I so desperately crave. A life with intimacy and passion. A life with someone I can laugh and cry with, instead of someone who only makes me cry. I want a partnership, a place to feel wanted and not just as a pretty face, but as someone with worth. I don't want to be ruled or shackled. I want what every girl wants; a fairy tale kind of love, pure and simple.

But that isn't the life I've been given. Not by a long shot. My life resembles a puzzle with missing pieces and no picture to go by. The constant struggle to hold myself together and find out who I really am. I've been on a leash for so long, I can't remember how to be anything other than the dutiful girl with no life of her own.

Who am I now?

I stare at the stark white walls of the living area and the mismatched, threadbare chairs that came with the place. I arrived with little more than the clothes on my back, and I've not bought a single thing since. Not one thing I can call my own. But where do I even begin? I've been told what to do and how to do it for so long, I don't know what I even like anymore.

Closing my eyes, I suck a breath in through my nose. The crashing waves sing to me, and I realise that's one thing I can be sure of; I like the ocean. It's peaceful and soothing, like the voice of an old friend. And at night, when the moon is high in the sky, it glistens as it sings its lilting lullaby. A twinkle of light in the darkness.

Like the dark eyes of the man who haunted my dreams the past few nights.

A man who by all rights should scare me to death. A man whose eyes seemed to devour me as they trailed the length of my body, awakening feelings that have been dormant for years. Not that I'd ever act on them. Jericho Lawson oozes power, and I've had about enough of living under someone else's reign. It's about time I got some of my own power back.

CHAPTER SIX

JERICHO

"You're sure that's the right place?" Tony leans his hands on the table, giving Zeb a pointed stare. "Because you have to be one hundred percent sure."

Zeb blinks profusely but nods. "I'm sure. I followed her back there and sat watching for two whole days. They never left."

Stubbs, one of the only other members to still be here from my old man's time, speaks up. "But are you sure that's the lab?" He flicks a toothpick between his teeth.

Zeb frowns, picking at his nails. "I mean, pretty sure, yeah. The windows are all blacked out, they open their windows wide late at night to let out smoke or whatever the hell it is. And there're all these dead plants dotted between the overgrown weeds." He glances to me. "That's what you said to look out for, wasn't it?"

I nod. "It is. You see anyone else go inside?"

"Just the guy. He was real cautious when she pulled up. Wouldn't open the door fully, kept looking around before he pulled her inside and locked the door."

"Sounds like our place."

Tony closes his eyes, massaging the bridge of his nose. "It does." He meets my gaze. "How do you want to proceed?"

"We know from last time that scaring them off doesn't work, they just come back and find another place out of the way." I pace the length of the room. "I think we need to do something bigger. Disable them permanently."

Tony's eyes widen and he holds his hands up. "Now wait a minute—"

"I'm not meaning disable *them*, but the lab. Make it so they can't just move on and start again. Make them think twice about setting up here."

Tony takes hold of my arm, pulling me aside. "I see where you're coming from, son, but is this really the way you want to go with it? What you're talking about is dangerous." He lowers his voice. "If this is about—"

I pull my arm from his grip. "Of course it is. It *always* is. I know they're not the ones who gave it to her or got her hooked, but they'll be the ones getting someone else's baby sister or brother into it, ruining their lives. You said yourself there was another death just the other day."

He nods. "I did. Which is why we need to move quick on this. But I need to know you can handle it."

"I can."

He nods then turns to Zeb. "Thanks, kid. You did good."

Zeb grins, his feet shuffling from side-to-side. "Thanks, Tony."

"Jericho's right. We need to make a stand, let it be known the Hellhounds don't tolerate methamphetamines in our town."

"What do you want us to do, boss?" Matiu swings back on his seat, his arms folded across his chest. "We ransacking their lab? A bit of snatch and grab?"

I shake my head. "I don't know if that sends a big enough message." I point at Zeb. "He already followed her outta town to buy the goods, so they're not afraid to do what needs to be done. No, I think we need to destroy the whole thing."

"Yeah, but destroy it how? We gonna blow the place up?" Matiu barks out a laugh, and I turn to Tony with a raised brow.

"Total annihilation," Zeb says with a firm nod.

Tony folds his arms across his chest. "It's risky."

"It sends a message, though," Stubbs agrees. Of all the guys here, he's the one I knew I could count on to see it from my point of view. He's old school. An eye for an eye is his motto, and he's been suggesting we strike harder for a while now. "They'd think twice about starting up again."

Matiu's face drops as he darts his eyes between the three of us. "Bro, you can't be serious."

Inhaling deeply, I rest my hands on the back of my chair, leaning my weight on it. "It's a lot, I know. But what choice do we have if we want it off our streets? The cops aren't doing shit about it, and we've already shaken down what, three others so far?"

"Yeah, but, Jeri, this is big time. We're talking about arson here, bro." He lets his seat legs swing back to the floor and clasps his hands on the table. "I don't wanna do time for these arseholes. Shiiiit. I'm too pretty for prison, and I ain't about to be anyone's spit roast."

Stubbs nudges him with his elbow.

"Neither am I, and if we do it right, we won't have to be."

"Okay, but what do you know about explosives?" Matiu leans forward. "I failed science at school. I don't know shit about it."

"Um, I can do it." Zeb steps forward, raising his hand. "I mean, I can probably get what you need and rig it up."

"You what?" Matiu grins, hooking his thumb over his shoulder at Zeb. "This fucking guy."

Zeb shrugs, grinning back. "My brother's in demolition. I helped him out a few times."

"That don't make you an expert." Tony steps in, placing his hand on Zeb's shoulder. "But I appreciate it, kid. You're willing to go the extra mile, and we can see that."

"Maybe we don't need some expert in blowing shit up. The fumes that come out of those places must be flammable as shit," Stubbs puts forward.

My brow furrows as I pace the room. I can't believe I'm even suggesting we do this bullshit or that they're taking it on board. This isn't what we do. This isn't who we are. The Hellhounds have avoided violence since my father was incarcerated.

Then why are we doing it now?

Kate.

I'm doing it for her and all the other Kates out there who don't have someone to keep them clean. I'm doing what I wish I'd done all those years ago when I first found out she was using.

"Maybe we could just Molotov cocktail the place," Zeb suggests. "You know, wait till no one is home and throw a fucking flaming bottle through the window."

Matiu cocks his head. "Kid might actually have a good idea there."

Minimises the risk, no one gets hurt, easy getaway. It's our best option so far.

"What do you think, Tony? Would be quick and easy. No casualties."

"Beats blowing our fucking fingers off trying to rig up an explosive we know jack shit about." Tony glances at Stubbs with a grin. "No offence."

Stubbs raises his right hand, offering the nub of his middle finger. "None taken, jackarse."

Tony chuckles then raises his gavel. "All those agreed?"

Everyone nods. "Yeah."

He brings the gavel down on the table. "Right, make it happen. Zeb, head back and keep watch. I want details of their movements. We might have an easy plan, but we're not going to go in half-cocked. I want no fuck ups, you understand?"

"Got it."

"We're not taking them out, just their lab. It could be days before they leave, but we need to be ready when they do." He levels Zeb with a stare. "Make *sure* no one is home before you give the call. I don't care if you have to sit there for weeks before you know their routine. No one gets hurt." He turns to Matiu. "You'll take care of the cocktail? Make sure it's ready to go when we are."

"On it."

"Good. Jeri, I'm trusting you to see this through. You keep an eye on them, look out for anything they miss. I do not want to be bailing your arses out of jail if this goes wrong."

"We've got this. Nothing will go wrong."

CHAPTER SEVEN

SAM

Pulling the door closed behind me, I step out into the sunshine and unlock the car. As I climb in, I glance through to the backseat out of habit. I don't know what I would do if there ever was someone hiding in there, but I check it all the same. I turn the key and glance up at my rearview mirror, taking one more precautionary look before pulling out of the drive and down the shingle road.

It's a bit of a hike back into town, and I usually use this time to think, but today I feel like listening to music. I flick through the stations until I find one with halfway decent tunes and reception that doesn't cut out every five seconds. Turning it up, I bop my head in time to the beat, tapping my fingers against the steering wheel. A smile tugs at my lips. Something so simple like picking the radio station shouldn't make me this happy, but it does. I am the one in charge now. I can make my own decisions.

I wind the window down and let the wind blow my hair about as I come up to the small rise before the long stretch of road that'll take me into the town centre. There's a sudden loud noise, and the car begins to smoke from under the bonnet. The temperature gauge is in the red. I manage to steer it to the side of the road before it dies completely.

"No, no, no, no, no!" I slam my hands on the steering wheel. "This can't be happening." I sit for a minute, unsure what to do. I try the key again and the engine rumbles back to life, but there's a rainbow of lights flashing on the dashboard and the temperature gauge goes right back up to the limit. Leaning my head back against the seat, I stare up at the roof. "What am I going to do?" I rummage through my bag for my phone to call Jen. I'm sure she would come and get me. No service flashes in the corner, and the battery light is on red.

Wrenching the door open, I pull myself out of the car and stomp to the front. I run my fingers underneath the bonnet to find the latch that opens it. With one hand holding it up high, I search for the little handle that should lock it in place, but there isn't one. Not that it would do any good anyway. I have no idea what I'm looking at. Slamming the bonnet back down, I brace my hands on the lid and take a few deep breaths. I'm going to have to walk.

Windows wound back up, doors locked, and reusable grocery bags under both arms, I set off down the road. Those grey clouds I was so sure would come have up and disappeared, and the sun beats down on my head as I make the slow trek into town.

About halfway in, I'm sure I can hear the distant rumble of an engine humming along the road behind me. For a brief moment I consider flagging the car down and asking for a ride, but self-preservation takes over and I move further to the side of the road. The air vibrates with the sound of what I can now tell is a motorcycle, and I quicken my pace. Sweat trickles down my back, and my breath comes in short pants as my chest tightens. I refuse to turn around even as the bike slows behind me. Whispering a silent prayer to the sky above, I force my legs to move faster, but they're no match for the motorcycle.

The engine revs, and then suddenly it's alongside me, pulling onto the grass verge on a diagonal.

"Everything okay?" the rider asks, and I have no choice but to stop.

I nod and hold up both thumbs. "Everything's fine."

He removes his helmet and hooks it under his arm, those familiar dark eyes finding mine. "You sure, princess?"

I nod again. "Mmhmm."

"That your car back there?"

My eyes follow where he's pointing, and I let out a sigh. "Yeah, it is."

"Want me to take a look at it for you?"

"Oh, you don't have to do that… I'm sure you have better things to do with your time." The grocery bags slip from my arm, and I scramble to grab them.

Jericho smirks. "You planning on walking all the way into town and then carrying your groceries all the way back home with you too?"

"I…" My mouth falls closed. He has a point. I didn't really think that part through.

"Look, I don't have any plans until later, and I'm happy to take a look and see if we can get you back up and running again, or I can give you a ride into town. Either way." He holds his free hand out to the side. "Offer's there if you want it."

I need a working car, and I don't know anyone in town other than Jen and Barb, and something tells me they wouldn't know the first thing about cars. And I really do need groceries if I'm going to eat this week.

"What'll it be, princess?"

With a resigned sigh, I nod, walking towards him. "Take me back to my car please. Maybe you can get it to work."

He hands me his helmet. "Thank you."

"No problem."

I swing my leg over the back, and he grabs my hands, placing them around his waist. My breath hitches and my heart pounds in my chest at the feel of his hands on mine. The firm muscles beneath my fingers seem to ripple as he kicks the stand and starts the engine, and I almost let go, afraid of the feelings coursing through me.

"Hold on tight."

CHAPTER EIGHT

JERICHO

"Who did you piss off?" I ask from under the bonnet.

"What? No one. Why?" Her voice shakes, and it's obvious she's lying.

"See this here?" I point to the large hose hanging loose behind the radiator. "That should be attached. Your car overheated because it has no water to cool it down."

"Could it have just fallen off?" There's a squeak in her voice as she asks, and it's about the cutest damn thing I've ever heard. It takes everything in me not to reach out and pull her into my arms.

Instead, I fix her with a stare as I wipe my hands on a rag. "Not likely, princess. So, I'm gonna ask you again. Who'd you piss off?"

She averts her eyes, looking anywhere but at me. A tell-tale sign she knows more than she's letting on. I was right. This girl is running from someone. Someone who clearly wants to fuck with her.

"I don't know anyone here." She shrugs, biting her lip, and damn if I don't want to run my thumb along the seam and tug it free. "Maybe it's just a prank?"

"All the way out here? I don't think so. Locals wouldn't venture this far for a prank." I slam the bonnet back down and walk around to where she's standing by my bike. "Look, I can reattach that for you, no problem, but you're going to need water to be able to drive it anywhere, and I don't have any on me."

Her eyes glisten with tears. "Okay."

Scanning the area, I don't see any houses close by, only farmland, but I know from Zeb the P lab isn't far. "You live around here?"

She points down the road. "Down by the beach."

Of course. Mr Garrison's place. That makes sense. Quiet place, out of the way, not in town where she'd stick out like a sore thumb. She's smart, but I can tell this has rattled her.

I motion towards my bike. "Jump on. I'll have one of the boys tow it back to yours and then I'll have you up and running again." Pulling my phone from my pocket, I find Cassian's number. Wetter behind the ears than Zeb, but good for a tow at least.

"You really don't have to do this."

"I think I do." I narrow my eyes as I glance back at her car and then towards the beach. It's a good ten kilometres from here. "You shouldn't be out walking by yourself. A lot of things can happen on a lonely country road."

Her eyes widen, and I curse myself for scaring her even further. "Not that Brookhaven isn't a safe place to live, but anywhere away from people isn't really safe for a woman to be by herself." *Jesus, now I sound like a sexist pig.*

"I can take care of myself."

"I don't doubt that for a second, princess. But judging by the shopping bags you were carrying, I'm assuming you were headed to town for groceries?" She nods. "That's another ten k, at least, into town, then twenty back to the beach carrying heavy bags." I let my eyes travel up and down her gentle curves. "No offense, but you look like you'd blow away in a strong wind."

She folds her arms across her chest defiantly. "I'm stronger than I look."

I believe her too. Whatever she's running from has her spooked, and even knowing there's a possibility of real danger, she's still determined to hold her own.

I reach out, brushing a wayward hair behind her ear. "You don't have to be strong all the time." Nodding towards the car, I say, "Fixing cars is my thing. Let me help you with this, and then I'll leave you to it."

"I don't know." She casts her gaze down the road in the direction she was walking then back at me. She's right to be cautious. She doesn't know me from Adam, and here I am, trying to convince her to get on my bike and go home with me. Alone.

I hold my hands up, palms out. "I promise, I just wanna help. No funny business." Anything to get her off this road and out of harm's way. There's no telling how many addicts race up and down this stretch of road to get their fix.

She pulls her lip between her teeth again, then nods. "Okay."

CHAPTER NINE

SAM

With the hose refitted and the radiator full of water again, Jericho checks over the rest of the car for any other signs of sabotage.

"Everything in order?" I ask, holding out a cup of coffee as he clicks the bonnet back in place.

"Seems to be, though it could do with an oil change." He holds his hands up in the air. "Could I use your sink to wash up?"

"Oh, of course." I lead him into the kitchen, placing his cup beside him. Rocking on my heels, I try to think of something else to say. "So, um, how do you know so much about cars?"

He chuckles. "It's a rite of passage in my family." I quirk a brow, and he continues. "I come from a long line of mechanics. It's in our blood."

"Oh right. That must come in handy."

"Pays the bills." He takes a sip of his coffee as his eyes scan the barren room.

I wave a hand at the emptiness, laughing nervously. "I haven't had a chance to decorate yet… new in town…" I bite my lip to stop myself talking. His eyes bore into my head as if he can read my thoughts. It's unnerving.

"What are you running from, princess?" he asks softly.

My head snaps up and coffee sploshes over the rim of my cup. "Shit." I reach for the dishcloth at the same time he does, and our fingers graze. A spark courses through my veins at the mere touch of his skin on mine, and I jerk my hand backwards, spilling more coffee.

"Here, let me." He takes my cup from my hand and places it on the counter, handing me the dishcloth to clean myself up.

"I'm such a klutz." I scrub at the coffee mark with the cloth. When the stain is as good as it's going to get, I glance back up to see him watching me. He's waiting for a response. "I'm not running from anything." My voice shakes so much, even I don't believe it.

"You live all the way out here by yourself, you have no personal effects around the place, you keep to yourself, and no one knows a thing about you. Sounds like you're running to me."

"You've been asking people about me?"

He smirks. "Brookhaven's a small place. People talk."

"Of course they do," I mutter under my breath.

"You in some kind of trouble?"

I purse my lips, furrowing my brow. I could lie to him and pretend everything is fine, but something tells me I can trust him. At least with some of it.

"I'm not sure. Maybe."

He folds his arms. "What does that mean? Maybe?"

Huffing out a breath, I sweep a hand through my hair. "It means I don't know. When I woke up this morning, the window was open." I meet his gaze. "But I could've sworn I closed it last night. I thought my mind was playing tricks on me, but now with the radiator hose…"

"You're not sure anymore," he finishes for me, and I nod. "I'm gonna ask one more time. Who're you running from?" He pushes aside the kitchen curtain, glancing out towards the drive.

I squeeze my eyes closed, dragging a shallow breath into my lungs. "My husband."

"Your husband?" He raises a brow, tilting his head. His eyes darken. "He hurt you?"

I duck my head, staring at the floor. "Not in the way you think. At least, not recently."

"What does that mean?" His voice is strained, his body taut with tension.

"It means he had other ways to hurt me. Under lock and key, isolated, curfew, constantly being watched, no privacy, no voice."

"He kept you prisoner?"

I think back to my spacious room at the compound. From the outside it looked glamorous, but in reality, it was anything but. Locks on the windows and doors, no human contact unless I was needed to be seen in the public eye. Guards stationed outside my door. "In a manner of speaking, yes." He quirks a brow, so I continue. "He had people to keep watch over me. Hannibal, his righthand man, was the worst. He could be kind one minute, then brutal the next. He did whatever Dante asked, no questions asked." I shudder and wrap my arms around my waist. "Dante was a cruel man, and Hannibal took pleasure from dolling out my punishments… I never really knew where I stood with him. At times, he was my worst nightmare."

"What does this Dante want from you?"

I laugh bitterly. "To take me back. Punish me." I shake my head, turning to glare out the window. "No one leaves Dante Costello unless he tells them to."

He steps towards me, his hand cupping my jaw. I close my eyes, leaning into his touch. "You're vulnerable out here by yourself, especially if he's tracked you down. And if what you said is true, it sounds like he might've."

I know he's right, but it doesn't stop the anger flaring in the pit of my stomach. Pulling back, I narrow my eyes. "And what am I meant to do? I have nowhere else to go. No money left to keep running."

"Let me help you."

"Help me? How? By making me a prisoner in my own home all over again? I don't think so."

"Woah. I didn't mean it like that." He fishes a card from his pocket, handing it to me. "At least take my number. You can call me anytime for any reason."

"Why? You don't even know me, and you have no idea what Dante is capable of."

He smirks. "I've been around the block a time or two, princess, I can handle myself just fine."

"You don't have to do this. It's not your burden."

"It shouldn't be yours either. Only a coward forces a lady to stay where she doesn't want to be." He nods at the card in my hand. "Look, you've got my number, use it if, and when, you need it. I'm going to take a quick walk around the house and check the place then I'll leave you to your day." He stalks towards the door, pausing before going through. "And bring your car into the garage on Monday, I'll give it a good service."

I open my mouth to speak but he's gone before I have a chance. Instead, I watch him out the window as he makes his way slowly around the house, checking windows and doors as he goes. I don't know if I made the right decision in confiding in him, but having a man like Jericho Lawson on my side can't be a bad thing. Can it?

CHAPTER TEN

JERICHO

Dante Costello. That name sounds familiar, but I can't figure out why. Whoever he is, he's a fucking low-life piece of shit. What kind of a mongrel keeps his wife prisoner and tortures her?

You know the kind. You lived with one.

She can deny it all she likes, but I don't buy that he didn't lay a finger on her. You don't go on the run and live like a hermit unless you're afraid of what will happen to you. And Sam is scared out of her mind.

The thought of anyone laying their hands on her sends my mind reeling. If there's anything I can't stand more than amphetamines, it's violence towards women.

It has nothing to do with them being the weaker sex or any of that bullshit—I've seen enough to know they're a damn sight tougher than most men—it's that they deserve to be shown respect. That's somebody's mother, sister, aunt. Women are the bringers of life, the nurturers, and they should be protected at all costs.

No one has the right to touch what isn't theirs, and certainly not when it's another's body.

Rage seethes through my veins as I rev the throttle, letting the land beside me fade into a blur. The hum of the engine beneath me isn't enough to soothe the anger flooding my body. I don't know if anything will.

As the landscape turns into houses and parks, I slow my bike, coasting through the streets until I reach Lawson's Lugs. Getting my hands dirty is about the only thing I know that can take my mind off things. It's the only thing that worked after my father went to prison, and the only thing that kept me sane after my mother and sister's passing.

Pulling the helmet from my head, I toss it over the handlebars and stalk inside, taking a detour through the hall to the photo of my grandfather. Benedict Lawson founded this place, turned it into what it is today. He combined his two favourite things; riding motorcycles and getting greased up under the bonnet of a car. Lawson's Lugs and the Hellhounds MC owe him everything.

With my palm pressed to the wall beside his picture, I tip my head back and stare at the ceiling.

"What do I do?" Raking a hand across my jaw, I let out a sigh.

"Everything okay, son?" Tony comes up behind me, offering a nod towards my grandfather. "Benedict." He slaps his hand on my shoulder. "You look like you could use a drink."

I crane my neck towards the bar, knowing it won't help the situation but wanting to do it anyway. "Yeah, I could." The call of the motors now forgotten, I follow him through the door and take a seat against the long mahogany bar.

Tony skirts around to the other side, pulling a bottle of Jack from the shelf and pouring two glasses. He pushes one my way, then rests his elbows on the bar. "What's going on?"

"You ever known someone was in trouble but didn't know how to help?"

His eyebrows rise slightly, and he tips his glass back, slamming it down. "You know I have."

I shake my head. "That was different."

"Was it?"

"He was your best friend; there wasn't anything you could do."

"I should've talked some sense into him. That's what I should've done, and that's on me. I have to live with that every day of my life." He pours another whiskey. "Eats me up inside what you went through."

"I wouldn't still be here if it weren't for you. You know that." I was fifteen when I found myself on his doorstep with my thirteen-year-old sister, Kate. My face was battered and bruised, and my shirt still had my mother's blood caked all over it. I hadn't been able to save her from him that time, and *I* had to live with *that* on my conscience.

"Still. I knew what was going down at yours. We all did. None of us had the balls to do anything about it, just turned a blind eye."

"He would've killed you if you'd tried."

"Better me than your angel of a mother." He stares into his glass, swirling the amber liquid. "May she rest in peace." He tips the glass back.

"The club needed you to live. Someone had to take over once he was gone."

"The club," he scoffs. "You needed your mother more than they needed me."

"What's done is done. We can't change that. You still kept me from going off the rails, and I appreciate that, because right now, I might need you to talk me off another ledge."

Tony stands up straight, a frown creasing his forehead. "What is it? You in some kind of trouble?"

"Not at the moment."

"But?"

"I may get myself into some."

"You're talking in circles, boy."

I huff out a sigh, raking a hand through my hair. "There's this new girl in town, works with Barb over at A Cut Above." Tony nods, listening. "I ran into her this morning, stranded out on Boundary Road."

"Car troubles?"

"In a manner of speaking. Her car had conked out, but only because someone had messed with it. And when I asked her about it, she said she thought someone had been in her house."

Tony leans back on his heels, shaking his head. "Jericho."

I hold up a hand. "Hear me out. The name Dante Costello mean anything to you?"

"It does. And it's nothing good. This girl is messed up with him?"

"She's *married* to him."

Tony lets out a low whistle. "Jesus, Jericho. You don't wanna get involved in that. Haven't you got enough on your plate right now?"

"The P lab is the least of my concerns at the moment. You said yourself he's not good news. And she's on the run and clearly afraid of the guy. Isn't there something we can do? Call in a favour?"

"That's a big ask for a girl you barely know."

"I know she's scared shitless, and I know she shouldn't be out there on her own. She's a bloody sitting duck."

"Jericho—"

"I know what you're gonna say, and you're wrong."

"I know you mean well here, son, but this ain't your fight. She's not for you to save."

"But what if she is? If we have any connection to this Dante guy, surely we can come to some arrangement with him."

Tony slams his hand down on the bar. "You don't make arrangements with Dante Costello. You stay the hell away from him. He has people everywhere, and he can get to you when you least expect it."

"I'm not afraid of an altercation."

"You should be. It's not just you he'll go after, it's everyone you've ever cared about."

Dragging my tongue along my teeth, I push up from the bar. "Well, it's a good thing most of them are dead already, isn't it?"

CHAPTER ELEVEN

SAM

"Well, if it ain't Jericho's princess." Matiu looks me up and down. "What'll it be, sweetheart?" He sucks on his tooth, folding his arms across his broad chest.

"Um, hi. Jericho said to bring my car in today?" I hook my thumb over my shoulder. "It needs a service."

He smirks. "I'll bet it does." He holds his hand out. "I'll need your keys."

"Oh, of course." I place them in his hand then step back, rocking on my heels. "Do I wait, or…" I purse my lips. Damn Dante for taking my life from me. I can't even do something simple like get my car serviced without being awkward. I don't know how to do anything in the real world.

Matiu chuckles, shaking his head. "You're out of your depth, ain't ya, sweetheart?" He nods towards the back of the workshop. "Go on out back. I'm sure Jericho will want to take care of this one himself." He cups a hand to his lips. "Yo, Jeri! You got company!"

I make my way to the rear of the building, and a door opens from an office to the side. My heart rate kicks up a notch as I take in the sight of Jericho leaning on the door frame. He's in dirty overalls slung low on his hips, the sleeves tied together at the front. A tight white singlet stretches across his chest, and I get a glimpse of the ink curling from his shoulder and chest and onto his back. My throat goes dry.

"Good to see you, princess. Glad you took my advice and brought your car in." He pushes off and saunters towards me with a lopsided grin. "We'll have you good and serviced in no time." He winks, brushing past me and taking the keys from Matiu, who looks on with amusement.

I stare at the spot of skin still warm from his touch, and heat pools in my centre. This man does things to me. He makes me feel things I shouldn't. Things I never thought I'd have the chance to feel. And I don't know what to do with that.

Jericho pulls up beside me and cuts the engine off. "Have you had any other troubles with it?" He unfolds himself from the driver's seat and makes his way to the front, lifting the bonnet and securing it with the rod I was apparently too blind to see on Saturday.

"Uh, no, nothing."

"Good." He pulls something long out from the engine and wipes it on a rag before inserting it again. "And what about other things?" He looks at me pointedly, his eyes piercing my soul.

"No." I shake my head. "Nothing."

"Good," he says again, turning back to the job at hand. He twists and tightens things, refills fluids, and then hoists the car up on two jack stands. Lying on a board with wheels, he disappears under the engine for a few minutes. He scoots back out, grabbing a tray that looks like it should be filled with paint, then slides straight back under again.

When he comes back out a second time, he wipes his hands on another rag, placing a plug on the ground beside him. "It'll take a few minutes to drain."

I frown, and my breath catches in my throat. "Is there something wrong with it?"

He pushes up from the ground, tucking the rag into his back pocket. "Nothing wrong. Just giving it an oil change, like I said."

"Oh, right."

He moves towards me, reaching his hand out before thinking better of it. "It's fine, honestly. I'd tell you if there was anything dodgy going on with it."

I let out a shaky breath. "Okay."

"Look, this is going to take a few more minutes. Why don't you head into my office and make yourself a coffee while you wait? I can come grab you when it's finished."

I nod, stepping into the crowded space. His desk is piled high with papers, and behind that sits a pinboard with even more tiny slips of paper attached. File boxes stuffed to the brim are stacked in the corner of the room. There's barely any room to move without tripping over something. It's chaotic. I don't see how he can get any work done in here.

Through the door beside his desk is a kitchenette with an L shaped bench. It's cluttered with dirty cups and spoons. There's a couch to the back of the room with a blanket thrown over the armrest. A coffee table sits in front with stacks of crinkled car magazines strewn haphazardly across.

I locate the jug and refill it before switching it on. After searching through the cupboards, I find no clean cups, so I fill the sink and get to work washing up.

By the time Jericho comes to find me, the dishes are washed, dried and put away, the bench is wiped down, and the magazines have all been stacked into a neat pile to one end of the coffee table.

His eyes sweep around the room before landing on me perched at the edge of the couch, flicking through a magazine. "You've been busy."

Heat rushes to my cheeks. "Uh, yeah, sorry. I hope it's okay. There weren't any clean cups, and once I got started..." I let my voice trail off, shrugging. "I thought it was only fair after you helped me out the other day."

"It was really no trouble, princess, but thank you for cleaning up. These guys wouldn't know a dish brush if it jumped up and bit them on the arse. You ever get sick of sweeping up old-lady hair, there's a job for you here." He chuckles, rasping a hand across his stubbled jaw. "Anyway, your car's all ready to go. Oil's been changed, tyres look good, and I've bled your brakes too. You shouldn't have any troubles with it."

"Thank you. I really appreciate it. I don't know the first thing about cars. Obviously."

"Well, as long as you don't go putting diesel in it, you really can't go wrong. But you ever have any concerns, bring it back in. I'll take care of you." He smirks, and damn if it doesn't make my legs turn to jelly. The idea of Jericho Lawson taking care of me shouldn't excite me as much as it does. I barely know this man, but already he's done so much more for me than Dante ever did. And I like it. I like it a whole lot.

CHAPTER TWELVE

JERICHO

Pulling into the carpark at Paparua Prison, a sinking feeling settles in the pit of my stomach. I promised myself I wouldn't come out here to visit him. Ever. Yet here I am, after fifteen years of no contact, about to face the man who ruined my life.

Tipping my head back, I let the warmth of the sun wash over me, but even that isn't enough to shake this ominous feeling.

What if he's still the same angry man he was all those years ago? Then again, what if he isn't?

I've spent my entire adult life trying to forget about him, trying to move on with my life and let sleeping dogs lie. There was a time, in the wake of Kate's death, that I considered coming out here and taking matters into my own hands. Thankfully, Tony was able to talk me down, make me see sense. As far as I'm concerned, he's my father, and this man is just the donor. The man who got my mum pregnant then turned into the angry, spiteful man I grew up with.

I take my time heading into the compound. Visiting hours don't start for another ten minutes, and there's already a line of people waiting to go in.

A lady with a baby in her arms eyes me warily, and I offer her a smile. She averts her gaze, lowering her face into the crook of the infant's neck as she takes a step closer to the door. I hang back, not wanting to worry her. I know I can be an intimidating presence, especially with my patch. Which reminds me; I need to remove my leather jacket. No gang paraphernalia allowed on prison grounds. Despite the Hellhounds being a club, the law doesn't see it that way.

The door buzzes and a warden unlocks the door, holding it open for the line to pass through. His eyes take in every person as they step across the threshold, watching for any contraband, no doubt.

I don't miss the added scrutiny I get as he zeroes in on my leathers thrown over my arm. Holding my hands up to show I'm carrying nothing else, I give him a smile and a nod.

The clerk at the desk takes down everyone's names and details, along with which inmate they're here to see. She takes phones, keys, wallets and places them in a cubby. Then one by one, everyone is ushered through the metal detector, and a few lucky patrons, like myself, get the pat-down treatment too.

We're led through an iron-barred gate, down a corridor, and through another locked door and told to wait in the meeting room. Various chairs and tables are dotted about the place, with guards stationed every few feet. Signs adorn the walls, warning of repercussions should we be found passing anything to the inmates.

After another ten minutes of waiting, a buzzer rings and the door down the far end of the room opens. Men in blue jeans and navy jerseys file through, their eyes searching for their loved ones.

I swallow the bile that tries to surface as I wait for him to see me, but the door closes and he's nowhere in sight.

I don't know if I'm more disappointed in him for not bothering to come out, or myself for believing he would. Once again falling into that same old trap where I assume he'll be the father he's meant to be. I should've known.

Taking a step back, I turn to the guard closest. "How do I get out of here?"

"There a problem?"

I gesture to the empty space around me. "Yeah, the person I came to see isn't here."

The guard raises his walkie to his lips, speaking quietly. There's a crackle of static, followed by one word. "Name?" He quirks his brow, obviously waiting for me to answer.

"Jericho Lawson. I'm here to see Jeremiah Lawson."

"One moment."

That moment stretches into a further ten minutes before the buzzer rings and a guard steps through the door. "Mr. Lawson?"

I step forward, raising my hand.

"Follow me." He turns abruptly and stalks through the door, marching down the corridor. The keys on his belt jangle with every step, bouncing against his thigh, and his shoes squeak against the polished floor.

We come to yet another iron-barred gate, and he unlocks it then gestures to the corridor to the right. "This way please."

He pushes through to a small room with a table and two chairs bolted to the floor. I frown, feeling suddenly like I've been dragged in for questioning. "What's going on?"

"You're here to see Jeremiah Lawson?"

I nod. "Yeah. Is everything okay?"

"He's been in solitary. He'll be along soon." And with that, he turns on his heels and leaves the room. He stands rigid against the wall opposite the door, keeping watch.

Solitary?

My shoulders hunch as a million reasons why he'd be in solitary flit through my head. Only one stands out. Same hot-headed idiot he always was.

I take a seat on the cold metal chair. It's flat and small and provides no comfort whatsoever. Whoever designed these clearly had quick visits in mind.

Clasping my hands on the table, I wait.

Another door opens and in shuffles a much older man, with a weathered face and tattoos up the back of his neck. His hair is no longer black, but silver and shaved short, and he sports a long goatee, but there's no mistaking him. Jeremiah Lawson, my father. He's dressed in the same blue as the rest, only his is more of an overall. His hands are cuffed together, as are his feet. If he's surprised to see me, he doesn't show it.

A guard follows him in, pushing him down into the chair opposite. His cuffs are attached to a bolt on the table and his feet to the legs of the chair.

"You've got five minutes."

The door closes behind him, and we're left in silence.

Jeremiah leans back in his seat, as much as he's able while bolted to the table, and regards me with a sneer.

"Fifteen years is a long time to wait for a visit, don't ya think?" He drums his fingertips against the table. "To what do I owe the pleasure, *son*?" He sucks his teeth in the way he always used to before he started cracking his knuckles. It was the first sign to keep your mouth shut and get out of his way.

"Believe me, I take no pleasure in being here."

Jeremiah snorts. "Still sitting up there on your high horse, I see."

"If trying to protect my mother and sister from your hands is sitting on my high horse, then yeah, I guess I am," I scoff. "Why were you in solitary?"

"Had to put someone in their place." He sniffs. "Guards didn't like how I did it."

"I see you haven't changed either. I don't know why I'm surprised."

"No point changing what ain't broke."

"This was a mistake. I don't know why I thought you could help me." I make to stand.

He gives me a scathing look. "Sit your arse down in that chair, boy. Fifteen years I been waiting for you to show your face, and I'll be damned if you're gonna walk out on me after thirty seconds."

With my palms flat on the table, I lean towards him. "You may have been able to control me when I was a child, but in case you hadn't noticed, I'm not that kid anymore, and I don't have to listen to your shit."

He raises his fingers in the air, almost in a placating manner, but I know better than that. "You're the one came all this way to see me, not the other way around, boy. You musta come for a reason, and by my reckoning, that means you *do* have to *listen to my shit.*" He smirks, resting his hands back on the table.

I twist my head to the side, taking a breath to calm myself before meeting his gaze once more. "What do you know about Dante Costello?"

His eyebrows rise, the smirk falling from his lips. "Now that's a name I haven't heard in a while. What kind of shit you got yourself caught up in?"

"I'm not caught up in anything."

"Ah." He grins lecherously. "This is about a woman."

I ignore his remark and continue. "What do you know about him?"

"I know he's not someone *you* wanna be messing with. You think I'm a piece of shit? Dante Costello makes me look like a fucking pussy."

Fuck. Tony was right.

"What's he into? Drugs? Guns?"

"All that and more. He has his finger in all the pies. Trafficking, whore houses, weapons, fucking everything." He raises his chin. "Whoever this woman is, she must have a pussy made of fucking gold to be worth going up against Dante."

My fingers curl into fists, and I have to force myself to take a step back so I don't do something stupid like get myself thrown in jail.

He smirks as his eyes flick from my fists to my face. "Still the same jumped-up shit you always were. What ya gonna do? Hit me?" He chuckles low in his throat. "You think you're ready to take on someone like Dante? All so you can be the big man and save one of his whores?" He shakes his head. "Didn't work out so well for you the first time. What makes you think it'd be any different this time?"

I'm in his face with the scruff of his overalls in my fist before I register what I'm doing. "She was not a whore!"

The door behind me swings open, and two firm hands grab my shoulders. "That'll do. Time's up."

I let go, holding my hands up as I step backwards. My father shoots me a sardonic grin. "Apple don't fall too far from the tree, does it, boy?"

CHAPTER THIRTEEN

SAM

Jen pops her head around the corner of the staffroom as I'm about to put my apron on. "How about a coffee run? I was running late this morning, and I haven't had my caffeine fix."

Hanging the apron back up on the hook, I grin. "Sure. What would you like?" I grab my wallet, but she waves me off.

"Put that away. My shout." She heads over to the till and pulls out a twenty, handing it to me. "Barb, you want anything?"

"Double shot espresso macchiato." She glances in the mirror. "Please."

"Ooh that sounds good. Get me one of those too and whatever you want for yourself. I've got back-to-back clients today, and I need something to keep me going." She rolls her eyes then winks. Her clients are like family to Jen, and she thrives on days like this.

I stroll down to the coffee shop on the corner, peering into the shop windows on my way. Aside from the coffee shop, grocery store and A Cut Above, I haven't ventured into any of the other stores around town. Ever since the car incident a few weeks ago, I've been reluctant to settle in and lay the foundations of my new life. As the days wear on and there are no more signs of Dante and his men, I'm beginning to think that maybe it might be okay to at least dip my toes in. Perhaps pick up a few creature comforts for my home; something to brighten the place up a little.

The coffee shop is busy, so I take my place in line and read over the menu. The now familiar roar of motorcycles rattles the shop windows as they pass, and I can't help the smile that forms on my lips. I haven't had to use Jericho's number, but knowing he's there makes me feel that little bit safer. In fact, it's because of him I'm feeling as though Brookhaven might just be the place I need.

I place my order and step to the side to wait. People bustle past outside the window. The Hellhounds have parked across the street and are converging on the corner. Jericho is in deep conversation with Matiu, his face set in a scowl.

"Order for Sam," the barista calls, and I turn away from the window, collecting the takeaway cups in a holder. I thank her then squeeze past the other waiting patrons.

Outside, the sun peeks out from behind the cloud cover, giving a hint of warmth to the cool day. I'm too busy enjoying the sun to notice the black SUV with tinted windows pull up beside me until I hear the door close and the clearing of a throat.

"Samantha." Hannibal nods his head, his hands clasped in front of him.

Flashing lights dance before my eyes, and the coffees slip from my grasp as I step backwards. "No," I whisper, closing my eyes. This can't be happening.

"You need to come with me." In one long stride he's beside me, his hand wrapped firmly around my upper arm. I cry out in pain, but he doesn't let up.

"Please," I beg, dragging my feet as he leads me towards the car.

"Boss man's orders."

"No!" I cry, wrenching with all my might to pull free. "I won't go back! Please, Hannibal."

His eyes soften as he looks at me, but he shakes his head. "Sorry." He yanks the back door open and pushes me inside. As he goes to close it, a hand clamps down on the edge and holds it open.

"Is there a problem here?" Jericho demands, his eyes narrowed in on Hannibal. Behind him stands Matiu and several other leather jacket clad men who look like they mean business. My body sags against the seat.

Hannibal flexes his neck and lifts the front of his jacket, showing off his gun. "No problem. Just taking her back where she belongs."

Jericho steps into Hannibal's face. "Seems to me the lady doesn't want to go with you." He drags his eyes from Hannibal's to meet my gaze. "You okay?" I nod, my lip trembling as I fight back the tears that want to fall.

Hannibal's shadow casts over me as he steps aside farther. "I obviously didn't make myself clear. She's coming with me."

"I don't think so." Jericho motions to Matiu, who moves around Hannibal with a glare on his face. He offers me his hand, which I take and allow him to pull me from the car. Instantly the men surround me, forming a barricade. "The lady stays."

Hannibal deliberates, his eyes flicking between me and the intimidating man in front of him. He tilts his head, holding his hands up, palms out as he steps backwards, a grin on his face. "No problem." His eyes find mine once more, and I know this won't be the end of it. Dante is coming for me, whether I like it or not.

CHAPTER FOURTEEN

SAM

Jericho wraps his arm around my shoulders and leads me into A Cut Above. Jen spins around, her smile falling from her face as she sees me. "My God, what happened?" She rushes over, taking me from Jericho and leading me to the couch. "You're white as a ghost."

"I-I dropped the coffee, sorry." My voice cracks.

"Oh, honey, that's okay. It's only coffee." She glances at the men standing outside the window, guarding the door. "Something tells me there's more than just spilled coffee on your mind."

Jericho crouches in front of me. "Was that him?" he asks softly.

I shake my head. "No, that was Hannibal. Dante doesn't get his hands dirty unless he has to." Tears fill my eyes. "He'll be back."

He places his hand on my knee, and the warmth helps to calm my racing heart. "And I'll be right here when he does."

"Who're we talking about? Someone explain what's going on, please." Jen straightens up, her arms folded.

Jericho holds my gaze, and I nod.

I need to come clean. "My husband, Dante."

"You're married?"

"Not by choice."

Jericho's eyes darken, and his grip on my knee tightens briefly.

"My father was a gambler. He owed a lot of bad people money. Dante was one of them."

"Oh Jesus," Jericho hisses under his breath. "Your own father sold you to a mobster?"

I look away, knowing how this sounds. "It was only meant to be for a year. I agreed to it at the time, but then he did something stupid, and Dante's son got killed. He swore he'd never let me go after that. An eye for an eye."

"Oh, honey. You've been working here almost a month now. Why didn't you say anything?" Jen perches on the edge of the couch. "We could've helped you."

I shake my head. "You can't help me. When Dante wants something, he gets it, whatever the cost. I wanted to protect you."

"And we want to protect you, chickadee. You're one of us now; we're not letting you go without a fight. Right?" She looks to Jericho who has the hint of a smile on his face as he nods.

"Right."

"I appreciate it, but I can't let you do that. The best thing for me to do is leave."

"Sure. You can leave. It's not safe for you to be all the way out there by the beach by yourself anymore."

"No, I mean I can't stay *here*, in Brookhaven. I need to get out of town."

"Well that's not happening. You can come live at the garage with me."

My eyes widen. "I'm not moving in with you!"

"Why not?"

"Because I barely know you." I shake my head. "I have to move on, away from here. He'll be back for me. It's not safe here anymore. For me or for you. It's better if I just go."

"But I don't want you to go. I like having you here at the salon. I'm not going to let some guy run off my best part-timer; husband or not." Jen huffs, looking to Jericho. "What if she comes to stay with me? I'm always up for company," she suggests. "It'll be like a sleepover."

"No." Jericho stands. "How would you protect her if Dante sends another of his goons to get her? She stays with me."

"But…"

"It makes sense, Sam." Jen nods her head. "Where else would you go? This is your home now. Let us help you."

"She's right," Barb says from behind the counter. "You can't let him chase you away."

I blink. "I didn't think you liked me."

She shrugs, her eyes rolling to the ceiling. "You're alright, I guess."

"It's settled then. Take the rest of the day off, get yourself all packed up." Jen turns to Jericho, placing a hand on his shoulder. "You'll go with her?"

"I won't let her out of my sight."

CHAPTER FIFTEEN

JERICHO

Sam paces back and forth in front of her kitchen counter. "I can't do this, Jericho. I can't be under lock and key again. I'm sorry." Her eyes glisten with unshed tears, and I want so much to take away the hurt.

"Hey." I reach out, taking hold of her shoulders and lowering my head to meet her gaze. "No one is locking you up."

She stops, placing her hands on her hips. "I won't let her out of my sight. That's what you said."

I rake a hand through my hair. She's right, I did say that, and I'm going to have to be more careful about what I say in front of her if this is going to work. I need her to trust me. "I'm not Dante. You won't be my prisoner. You'll be free to go however and whenever you please, but at least living with me in town there's a better chance one of us will be there if you need us. Safety in numbers."

She lowers her eyes, picking at the hem of her top. "It would be easier for everyone if I just left." Her voice is small, broken.

"Not everyone." With two fingers under her chin, I bring her face level with mine. "It's not easier for you." I don't mean to do it, but my eyes flick to her lips and back up. I've wanted to kiss those lips since the first moment I laid eyes on her. "And it's certainly not easier for me."

When her tongue darts out to wet her lips, I'm done for. Slowly, cautiously, I tilt her head further back, lowering my forehead to rest on hers. Her lips part and her eyes flutter closed, and I lean in, brushing my lips over hers in a tender kiss. It's brief, but it's all I dare do right now.

"Let me do this for you." I search her eyes, seeking permission. "Let me keep you safe."

"But what if you can't?" she whispers. "You don't know what he's capable of. He could go after your family, the Hellhounds' families, Jen, Barb... He'll find the weaknesses and he won't stop until he has what he wants." A sob catches in her throat.

"He can try, but he won't get very far. The Hellhounds *are* my family, and they'll fight for what's right if it comes down to it. And holding you hostage isn't right." I let my hands slide along her jaw, cupping her face gently. "You're in Brookhaven now, princess. You're one of us, and we protect our own." She frowns, and it occurs to me I'm doing exactly what Dante did; giving her no choice. Letting my hands fall to my sides, I huff out a sigh. "But if you really want to leave, I won't stand in your way." I take a step back, shoving my hands into my pockets. "It's your decision."

She pulls her lip in between her teeth, and I can tell she's torn between doing what she *thinks* is the right thing, and doing what she *wants* to do.

"You promise you won't keep me locked away?"

I hold up three fingers. "Scout's honour."

That makes her lips tug up at the corners. "And if things get worse, you'll let me leave if I want to?"

I grit my teeth. "If it's what you really want to do, then yeah, you can leave. You're in control here."

She pulls her lips in tight, her eyes darting about the room as she thinks it through. Finally, she gives a small nod. "Okay. I'll do it."

CHAPTER SIXTEEN

SAM

"Here you go." Jericho swings the door open and steps aside. I walk up the narrow stairs to the apartment above the garage with Jericho following behind. I wait on the landing as he unlocks yet another door. His hand settles on the small of my back as he ushers me in. "It's not much, but it's home."

The room is bright, sun streaming in through two large windows overlooking the main road. Two worn leather couches sit against the back wall, and framed pictures of bikes and classic cars hang above. A La-Z-Boy recliner sits on an angle facing the large flat-screen TV. There is a coffee table made from a car engine with a sheet of glass over top, littered with magazines and greasy engine parts.

"Lounge, kitchen." He points as he leads me through the space, and I can't help but notice the similarities between his office and home. Dishes stacked haphazardly on the benches—though these, at least, seem to be clean—pantry door wide open with all manner of things scattered throughout. The place is in desperate need of a woman's touch.

He directs me towards the hall. "Bathroom, toilet." We stop outside another door. "And this is my room. You can put your things in here."

I raise a sceptical brow. "Excuse me?" Glancing back down the hall, it becomes obvious there are no other rooms but this one. "You want me to share your room?" My voice squeaks. We had a moment back at my place, but that's all it was; a moment. I'm in no way ready to play house with a man I barely know.

He chuckles, bringing a finger to smooth the crease in my brow. "Don't get your panties in a knot, princess. I'll be on the couch."

He turns and saunters back the way we came.

"Wait, what?" I drop my bag and reach for his arm. "I'm not kicking you out of your room, Jericho."

His eyes dance as he licks his lips. "That your way of telling me you wanna share?"

Heat burns my cheeks, and I swallow. "Um, n-no that's not what I meant." He steps in closer, and I lose all train of thought.

"Sure sounds like that's what you meant." His fingers brush under my chin, and I close my eyes, tilting my head ever so slightly. His hand slides around to the back of my neck, tangling in my hair as he grips my waist with the other. He crushes me to his chest, his breath warm against my cheek before his lips find mine. It's soft at first, gentle, like he's afraid he'll break me, and I suppose he has every right to think that way. I'm damaged goods, broken at the hands of a tyrant.

I sigh into his mouth, running my hands up his broad chest and around his neck. I press myself closer, pulling him towards me with a force I didn't know I had in me. He growls against my lips, and my back hits the wall behind me. He slides his hand down over my arse, to my thigh, pulling it up to meet his hip.

Every cell in my body is alight with a fire that had been all but extinguished years ago. It roars to life at the touch of his hands, the flames licking my wounds, helping me forget what's at stake. Staying in Brookhaven is risky, but it's a risk I'm willing to take if it means even one more second of feeling like this. Of feeling free.

I grind my hips into his, and his hand circles around to my throat, his fingers gripping my jaw. A flash of another time and place hits me square in the chest, and chills run down my spine. My blood turns to ice in my veins, and I whimper. My hands fall to the front of his shirt, gripping the fabric and simultaneously pushing him away and pulling him close.

He holds his hands up, taking a step back. "Shit, sorry. I got carried away. I didn't mean to—"

I shake my head, folding my body in half as I brace my hands against my knees. My chest feels as though it's in a vice, and I can't seem to get enough air in.

"Hey." He drops to his knees, peering up at me. "What do you need?"

"I… I don't…" I clutch at my throat, tears stinging my eyes.

"Shhh, it's okay. Look at me, Sam." He takes hold of my shoulders and guides me to the floor. "Look at me." I obey without a second thought. "Breathe with me, okay? In, two, three, four… out, two, three, four."

I focus on the way his shoulders rise and fall with each breath and try to emulate it with my own. Breath by ragged breath, I drag myself back from the depths of my jaded memories. My cheeks heat, and I drop my head to rest on my knees. "I'm so sorry," I whisper.

Jericho moves his hands from my shoulders, and there's a shuffling sound as he plants himself beside me. His head hits the wall with a light thud. "You've got nothing to be sorry about, princess. I never should've pushed you like that. I'm the one who should be sorry."

I turn my head to peer at him. "You weren't to know. *I* didn't even know I'd—" I search for the right words, "—*panic* like that."

"After what happened today, I'm not surprised. It must've brought up some feelings." He frowns, scrubbing a hand across his jaw.

He's right, it had, but that doesn't excuse my reaction. Jericho has gone out of his way to help me on more than one occasion. In fact, it's becoming somewhat of a habit of his. To fear him makes no sense, and yet, when he'd placed his hand around my throat, fear is exactly what I'd felt.

His dark eyes stare into mine, and he lifts his hand slowly, tentatively. With a touch so gentle, he brushes my hair from my face. "I'm sorry, princess. It won't happen again. I want you to feel safe here."

A pang of something—sadness maybe—hits me in the stomach and swirls around, making my head spin. I might not be ready to play house with him, but I don't want him to keep his distance either. I *want* him to be near me, touching me. And that revelation has that swirl turning into a swarm of butterflies in my stomach. I haven't wanted a man to touch me in the longest time, and here I am, not only trusting my life in this man's hands, but actually wanting *more* from him.

Dante may have been my downfall, but it's Jericho who will be my undoing.

CHAPTER SEVENTEEN

JERICHO

Stupid, stupid, stupid.

How could I be so stupid? She told me what she's been through. I *know* from the look in her eyes and her determination to flee to keep everyone else safe, she's been through a lot. More than anyone should ever have to go through. And even knowing that, I *still* make the monumental fuck up of putting my hands on her. No, not just on her, but around her fucking throat. Of all the things I could've done, why did I go for the throat? What the fuck did I think was going to happen? She'd forget all about her abuse and give herself to me?

Jesus Christ, you're an idiot, Jericho.

I've single-handedly fucked up the first relationship I've wanted in years, before it even began. It had barely made it off the ground, merely hovering a few fragile millimetres before it crashed and burned.

I huff out a breath, throwing my arm over my face. She's probably going to leave now. I'll come home from work tomorrow to an empty apartment, and it'll be all my fault.

And even knowing that, I can't get the taste of her lips out of my head. The feel of her skin against mine, the way she sighed into my mouth… It's enough to drive a man insane. She's soft and delicate to the touch, but there's a strength in her, a fight that I'm drawn to. It doesn't take a genius to work out why. She reminds me so much of her. The way she'd rather suffer in silence than drag everyone else down with her, or the way she's stubborn and resolved to be independent, not wanting to burden others. The one difference is that she got out before it was too late, and unlike my mother, she has people in her corner willing to fight alongside her.

I was fifteen when I attempted to stand up to my father and take the blows instead of her. I was fifteen and had to watch as he beat her to death because I dared stand in the way. I was fifteen when I lost both my parents in one night and realised I wasn't as strong as I thought.

But I'm not fifteen anymore, and I'll be damned if I let another man take away the life of a woman who could flourish without his thumb holding her down. If Sam wants to leave after what I did, I wouldn't blame her, but I won't give up trying to help her. I can't. I couldn't live with myself if anything were to happen to her. Not when it's within my power to stop it.

Lying here in the dark, knowing she's only a few steps down the hall; it kills me. Is she packing already? Is she sinking into a black hole of dread, wondering what she got herself into?

I'd give anything to go to her, to make sure she's okay, that I haven't opened old wounds. But something tells me that would be the wrong play. As much as I want her to feel safe with me, I also want her to *want* to be here. And that means I can't keep pushing it. After what Dante did to her—because even though she hasn't said it in so many words, I *know* what he did—I have to hand her the control. Show her I'm not like him. If there's any chance in hell she'll forgive me and be willing to give this a go, she has to come to me, not the other way around. I need to take a step back.

I can do that. It won't be easy, but I can do it.

CHAPTER EIGHTEEN

SAM

Staring at the ceiling after a restless night's sleep, I go over the events of yesterday. Dante's reach is far and wide, and I have no doubt in my mind that he'll be back. The question is when. He's not one to play games, and he certainly doesn't like to lose face. I hate to think what Hannibal faced upon his return without me in tow, but it's the price you pay for getting into bed with a criminal. I should know.

Once again, I find myself full of a bitterness towards my father and his foolish antics. If it wasn't for him and his addiction, I never would've been in this position in the first place. What kind of father sells his own daughter to pay his debts? And as if that wasn't enough, when I was mere months from freedom, he ripped the very essence of my being from my chest all over again, leaving me chained to my captor for the rest of my days. And to think, I once idolised him. I dreamt of marrying a man just like him. Daddy's little girl.

What would he think of me now, I wonder? On the run from one man while shacked up with another. Not exactly how I'd envisioned my life going, and one would hope it wasn't in his plans either. But then again, he's the reason I'm in this mess in the first place, so who knows. Perhaps it's all part of some master plan I wasn't made privy to.

Huffing out a sigh, I roll to my side and attempt to shake away these thoughts. There's no point dwelling on something I can't change. The only thing acceptable is to make the most of a bad situation. At least I have a roof over my head and a job I enjoy. And, if I'm honest, I finally feel like I have the makings of a life here in Brookhaven. The people here have taken me under their wings and made me feel welcome. More so than I probably deserve. I didn't exactly put myself out there when I arrived, and though I'd tried to keep my distance, they somehow managed to weasel their way into my heart anyway.

Especially the man sleeping on the couch down the hall. He'd flat out refused when I offered to sleep out there instead, claiming that he was the first line of defence if anyone did try to break in through the night. And I suppose he has a point, but it doesn't make me feel any better about it.

He's upended his life for me without so much as a bat of the eye. Taking me in, giving up his personal space, and virtually becoming my live-in bodyguard all at the drop of a hat. I've never known anyone like him before. Where I'm from, everyone is out for themselves. Even Hannibal, Dante's right-hand man. Sure, he does as the boss bids, but it's for his own benefit. Being Dante's number two has its perks, and it grants him certain freedoms the other lackies aren't afforded; his own private wing at the compound, a hefty salary, and the promise of one day taking over the business.

With no heirs to the throne, so to speak, Dante will have no choice but to hand everything over to the only man he can trust to never betray him. He's made a lot of enemies over the years, and there are many who would like to see him fall from his perch. Hannibal is the only one to remain loyal throughout the years, and it's no surprise given Dante took him under his wing as a young boy, teaching him the ways of the business and giving him a life he could only dream of. He'd been plucked from the streets, a grubby kid with barely a cent to his name and no family to speak of, and for that, Hannibal remained his ever-loyal servant, though he did have a softer side that would come out on occasion.

Thrust into life as a surrogate mother to a man only a few years my junior, I'd made it my duty to form a bond with him, hoping he would help me escape when the time came. I'd been mistaken. His loyalty to Dante ran far too deep for even me to penetrate. He could be ruthless and cruel. But every now and then he would show me mercy. Whether it was out of boredom or a macabre way to toy with my emotions, he would show me a softer side, passing pieces of poetry through the small gap under the door. Though he'd been a part of my torment, he'd also given me hope when I'd felt all was lost.

And now, he'd been tasked with the duty of bringing me back to the man of my nightmares. The man who shut me away and took all my freedoms from me. The man who, if he'd had his way, would've fathered my children to create the heirs he so desperately wanted. The man who forced himself on me, time and time again, not knowing that what he wanted was nigh on impossible. Thank you, polycystic ovarian syndrome.

With my hand on my stomach, I suck in a deep breath and let it out slowly before pushing myself up out of bed. I've wasted enough time reliving the past.

I grab my dressing gown and push my arms through as I ease the door open and peer down the hall. No sign of life. I tiptoe to the bathroom to freshen up, splashing water on my face and brushing my teeth. I make my way out to the darkened lounge to find an empty couch and a note on the coffee table.

Gone down to the garage to open up.
Help yourself to breakfast. Call me if you need anything. I'll be back for lunch.
Jericho

In the kitchen, I pull the curtains open to let the sun in. I fill the jug to make a coffee, and then turn to the bench of dishes. Shaking my head, I drag my sleeves up my arms and set to work cleaning up while I wait for the jug to boil.

After opening several cupboards and drawers, I manage to find where everything goes. It's not hard; there's barely anything in them. One large frying pan that sees a lot of use, a mismatched set of cooking utensils in one drawer, and a lone can opener in another. I've heard of minimalist living, but this is ridiculous.

At least the pantry shelves and fridge are stocked with food. I whip up a quick breakfast, then scour the shelves for something to make for Jericho when he comes home for lunch. It's the least I can do.

With a frittata in the oven, I settle myself on the couch, curling my feet beneath me and wrapping a blanket over my legs. I grab my worn copy of *Little Women* and turn to the bookmarked page. It had been my favourite book growing up, and it offers comfort to my days when so much of my time is spent in unease.

The thud of footsteps climbing the stairs outside sets my heart to racing until a faint jangle of keys rings out and the door is unlocked. Jericho steps in, his eyes finding mine with a look of surprise. The corner of his lip quirks up into a boyish grin, and I can't help but return it.

"Busy morning, princess?" He nods at the book in my hands.

"Very." I slot my bookmark back in and set the book aside, swinging my feet to the floor. "You hungry? I made lunch." I pad into the kitchen and pull the oven open, the smell of eggs, bacon and cheese wafting out and making my stomach grumble.

"That smells amazing. But I didn't expect you to cook for me. That's not why you're here." He comes up behind me, his head peering over my shoulder. His face is so close, if I turned my head a touch, I'd be able to kiss him.

Heat radiates through me as thoughts of the previous evening come flooding back. His hands on me, his lips against mine. Jericho Lawson has the power to drive any woman to the brink of insanity with just one smouldering look.

As if he can read my thoughts, he takes a step back.

I clear my throat. "Uh, yeah, I know. I just wanted to do something nice for you. To say thank you… for all this." I step aside, gesturing to the room around us. Being so close to him does something to my brain and makes it hard to think.

"Well, thank you, princess. I appreciate it." He stalks to the pantry and pulls out two plates. "Haven't had a woman cook for me since I left home."

I snort in a very unladylike fashion then quickly cover my nose with my hand. "I find that hard to believe." Heat swarms to my cheeks, and I know my face will be a lovely shade of red right now.

Jericho smirks, his eyes dancing with amusement. "You calling me a liar?"

My eyes widen, and I shake my head. "No! Of course not. I would never…" I ramble some incoherent words, and Jericho barks out a laugh.

"Relax." He brings a hand up to cup my cheek, rubbing his thumb along my jaw. Closing my eyes, I lean into his touch. "You don't need to be nervous around me. I don't bite."

"I'm not." The words come from my lips, but they're a lie. I *am* nervous around him. And not just because he's a man I barely know from Adam, but because he makes me feel things I have no right feeling.

He chuckles, pulling his hand from my cheek and turning to the food. "Whatever you say, princess."

My face feels bare without his hand there, and I replace it with my own, but it's not the same. His offers comfort and safety, while mine only offers fear.

He hands me a plate, leaning his hip against the counter. "I have a meeting in town after lunch, but I can send Matiu up to stay with you and keep watch."

"Oh no, you don't have to do that." The last thing I want is to upheave his work as well. "I was going to pop into the salon and see if they needed a hand."

Jericho frowns. "Is that a good idea? Hannibal could still be in town. He could be watching the salon for his moment." He puts his plate on the bench and dusts his hands down his thighs. Pulling his phone from his back pocket, he says, "I can reschedule my meeting and go with you."

"No." I place my hand over his. "Please, Jericho. You've already done so much for me. I don't want to get in the way of your work too."

"It's no big deal."

"It *is* a big deal. It's a huge deal what you're doing for me." I take a breath. "I'll go straight from here to the salon and I won't leave until they close, then I'll come straight back, okay?"

His eyes search mine, and finally, he relents. "I don't like it, but I guess I can understand it." He points a finger at my chest. "Just… call me if there's even a hint of Dante or Hannibal sniffing around, okay?"

I nod. "I promise."

He holds his hand out. "Gimme your phone."

"What for?" I ask as I hand it over.

"I'm putting Matiu's number in here too, just in case. If, for whatever reason, I don't pick up, you call him straight away. The boys know to keep an eye on you."

My heart jumps into my throat. The more people who know, the more people are in danger. "Did you tell them why?"

"Of course not. All they know is you're under my protection after what happened with Hannibal. That's all they need to know for now." He presses two fingers beneath my chin and tilts my head up, so I'm forced to meet his gaze. "They're not idiots though. It won't take them long to piece it together."

Tears well in my eyes as I nod. I was stupid to think they wouldn't all be involved somehow. Not only was I putting Jericho, Barb, and Jen in danger, but his whole club.

I should never have accepted their help.

CHAPTER NINETEEN

SAM

Jericho goes down before me, checking the coast is clear before he ushers me out. It all seems surreal that this is my life now. I've been on the run, living a life of solitude for so long, that it feels strange to have someone else taking some of the pressure off me.

It also makes me aware I can't let my guard down. These people have taken me in and taken on my burdens as their own; the least I can do is keep myself out of trouble when they're not around.

I place my hand on Jericho's arm as I pass him. "I'll be fine."

He folds his arms across his chest, watching me as I climb into the car. I adjust my mirror and check the backseat. When I'm satisfied all is well, I turn on the ignition and put the car into gear. I wave as I pull the car around to head out the drive down the side of the building, and Jericho stays watching, his eyes piercing.

The roads are quiet for a Friday afternoon, and I easily find a park out back. Grabbing my bag, I slip in through the back door.

Jen pops her head through the salon door. "Oh, it's you." She smiles. "What are you doing here? You're not rostered on today." Her face pales, and she steps through the door, lowering her voice. "Is everything okay?"

I silently curse myself for not calling first and worrying her. "Everything is fine, Jen. Sorry, I didn't mean to scare you. I just thought I'd pop in and see if you needed a hand with anything?"

Jen smirks, folding her arms across her chest. "Going stir crazy already, chickadee?"

My shoulders loosen as I chuckle. "That obvious, huh?"

"Just a bit. Not that I blame you. It can't be easy moving in with someone you just met." She places her hand on my arm. "Seriously though. How're you holding up? You really scared me the other day."

Tears prick my eyes and my bottom lip trembles. It's been too long since I've had friends or any semblance of normalcy. "Sorry."

"Hey, you've got nothing to apologise for." She rubs her hand up and down my arm. "This is not your fault, chicken."

"I know, but I shouldn't have led them here... to you. You're all in danger now."

Jen waves a dismissive hand through the air. "Pfft. Don't you worry your pretty little head about any of us, okay? Jericho and the gang… *club*—" she glances towards the salon, where I'm sure Barb is listening, "—won't let anything happen to any of us." She tilts her head to meet my gaze. "This is their town, and they don't take too kindly to outsiders stepping on their toes."

I huff out a laugh. "I'm an outsider too, Jen."

"Aww, honey, no you're not." She wraps a comforting arm around my shoulder and leads me to the door connecting the staffroom to the salon. "You see that door out there?" She points a manicured finger to the front of the building. "The minute you stepped foot through there, you became one of us. And nothing those thugs do or say is going to change that. Okay?"

I snivel, nodding my head.

"I mean it. Even if you weren't Jericho's girl—"

Her words fade into the background. *Jericho's girl?* Is that what I am? Heat pools in my cheeks as I remember the kiss from last night. Perhaps I *am* Jericho's girl.

"Chicky?" Jen's concerned face jumps into my view. "You still with me?"

"Oh, sorry." I grimace, offering up a shrug. "I'm away with the fairies."

"Listen to me waffling on." Jen laughs, her bracelets jangling as she tucks her red braid behind her back. "Look, it's a slow day today, so why don't I give you a hair treatment?" She pushes me into one of the reclining seats by the sinks. "I think you could use a little pampering."

Barb rolls her eyes as she folds the foils over on Mrs Trembath's hair. "Never offers to give me a treatment," she mumbles under her breath.

Jen juts her hip out, pointing a comb in her direction. "Honestly," she says in exasperation. "The second you find yourself in a dire situation, I'll give you some pampering too. It's not like I haven't done it before." She shakes her head, tsking under her breath.

Barb snorts derisively as she brushes more dye over the thick greys and wraps a strip of foil over top. Holding Mrs Trembath's gaze, she winks. "I belong to a motorcycle *gang*, Jen, remember? My whole life is a dire situation."

Mrs Trembath brings her hand to her lips, talking in an exaggerated whisper as she returns the wink. "It does sound rather dire, if you ask me."

"Now you're turning on me too, Judy?" Jen says in a tone that lacks conviction.

Judy's hand flutters to her chest in mock outrage. "I wouldn't dream of doing such a thing."

"I should hope not." Jen clucks as she turns on the faucet and tests the water. "You're one of my favourite clients." Cupping her hand around her mouth, she whispers, "Don't tell the others I said that."

Judy pinches her fingers together and runs them across her lips. "Your secret is safe with me."

Glancing at the clock on the wall, Jen sucks her teeth. "Oh what the hell. Once you're finished there, Barb, pop yourself in that chair and I'll give you a treatment while we wait." She turns to Judy. "You can have one too once we wash that colour out."

Mrs Trembath beams. "Oh, how lovely. You're a gem." She meets Barb's eye, and they share a conspiratorial grin.

"The things I do," Jen mutters as she leans me back until my head hangs over the basin. The warm water washes over my scalp, soothing my busy mind as her fingers rake through my hair. Closing my eyes, I listen to the music playing over the speakers and let my mind shut off for a moment. Jen's fingertips gently press into my scalp, massaging. It's heavenly, blissful, and oh so relaxing. All the stresses and worries of the previous days ebb out of my body as I succumb to her magic touch.

"So," Jen says, breaking the quiet, "what's it like living with a man like Jericho? He looking after you all right?"

"It's…" *Tempting, distracting, way too easy.* "Different." I peel my eyes open, catching her gaze with an awkward shrug. "I haven't lived with anyone else in months, and even then, I was kept locked away. I guess I'm not used to having someone in my space."

"It'll take a bit of getting used to, I suppose. He's being a gentleman?" Her fingers pause, and she raises a brow at me.

"Oh yeah, of course. He slept on the couch." I don't tell her what happened before that, or how I considered tiptoeing out to him during the night. After the way I reacted to him, I doubt he would've welcomed my advances even if I'd had the nerve.

"I give it a week."

"Barb! Give the guy some credit." Jen shakes her head. "He's doing this out of the goodness of his heart."

Barb snorts as she takes a seat beside me. "Says the woman who insists on calling the Hellhounds a gang." She throws an apron across her front, securing it behind her neck. "Yes, I heard you."

"Slip of the tongue." Jen waves a hand through the air. "Either way, he's a decent guy helping out a damsel in distress." She winks. "He's like your own Prince Charming, right, chicken?"

"Are we talking about the same guy? *Charming* is not the word I'd use to describe Jericho Lawson." Barb leans back, nestling her neck into the groove above the sink. "He *is* a decent guy. I'm not denying that. But he's not all sunshine and rainbows. He has a past."

Jen waves her hand through the air. "Don't we all?"

Barb inspects her nails, picking at a tag of skin beside her thumbnail. "I suppose we do." She gives me the side eye, sighing as if it hurts her to say it. "I guess he could be some form of knight in shining armour, or whatever you're into. The way Matiu tells it, Jericho's got it bad for our little runaway."

My throat goes dry. *Jericho has it bad? For me?*

"And who could blame him? She's a catch." Jen squeezes my arm.

"I think our definitions of a catch differ somewhat." *Broken, tainted, unworthy.* No matter how much I'd like to make things work with Jericho, I know

I'll never be what he deserves. I'm used goods. Tired and a little worse for wear. I'm nobody's catch.

CHAPTER TWENTY

JERICHO

"Is it true?" Tony levels me with a stare as I shut the door behind me. I've been busy with the garage and meetings and haven't had a chance to fill him in on anything, but it seems someone has bet me to it.

"If you mean did I ask Sam to move in with me, then yes, it's true." I fold my arms across my chest, standing firm.

"Jesus Christ, Jericho. I told you to leave it alone, not invite the goddamn enemy inside." He points a finger out the door. "You realise you've jeopardised every one of those men out there?"

I shake my head. "Sam is not the enemy here. Dante is. And I haven't asked them to do anything they wouldn't do of their own accord. They don't know who she's running from, only that she needs protection." I lean forward, planting my palms on the table. "Isn't that what we do? Offer protection when it's needed? Keep the streets clean?"

"This is different, and you know it. This isn't about keeping the streets clean, this about you and your father."

I duck my head, my shoulders bunching around my neck. "This has nothing to do with him."

"Oh really? You wanna tell me why you went out to see him then?"

My head snaps up, and he nods. "Yeah, I know about that."

"It was a mistake. I went to see what he knew about Dante because you wouldn't tell me anything useful." It's a low blow, and I know it.

He juts his chin out. "And did he offer anything different?"

I huff out a sigh. "No."

He stalks around the table, leaning his hip against the edge and folding his arms. "I would've come with you if you'd asked."

Keeping my eyes downward, I nod. "I know."

His hand falls on my shoulder. "I know that must've been hard for you." He drops his hand. "I thought prison would've changed him, made him regret his actions, but…"

"He's still the same."

"Yeah, he is." He inhales deeply, bringing his finger and thumb to the bridge of his nose. "I don't want the same thing for you, Jericho. I know you, and I know if push comes to shove, you'll defend her with everything you have in you, but at what cost?"

I meet his gaze. "I don't care what cost. I couldn't save my mother, and I wasn't there for Kate when I should've been, but I can make amends here. I can do for Sam what I couldn't do for them."

"Nobody can fault you for that, son, but how much do you really know about this girl? Do you really want to throw your life away to save someone you barely know?"

"What you did for me and Kate; taking us in, providing for us; I can't thank you enough for it, but it still doesn't take away the fact that my life was lost a long time ago. He made sure of that." My jaw clenches as my father's smirking face flashes across my mind. "I don't want that for Sam. I want her to live freely, without the need to run from town to town. And if I have to give my life to ensure that happens, I'll do it."

Tony closes his eyes, sucking in a breath. "You understand how crazy that sounds? You're willing to give your life for this girl you've known for what? A few weeks? A month at the most? And what about them, huh?" He points out the door again. "Those men out there will follow you anywhere you tell them to go, you know that. Hell, they'd follow you even if you told them not to. This is a brotherhood, Jericho. We stick together, no matter the cost, and you're going to drag them down with you."

"No, I'm not. The only one who knows the full story is Matiu; the rest are in the dark, and I'm going to keep it that way as long as I can."

He shakes his head. "You're fooling yourself if you think you can keep this from them. You're forgetting how small this town is and how fast word spreads. By keeping her here, you're putting everyone at risk. You want that on your conscience?"

Raking a hand across the scruff on my jaw, I let out a ragged breath. "You know that's not what I want. The Hellhounds mean the world to me."

"But you're choosing her over them."

"Why does it have to be a choice?" I demand, slamming my hand on the table. "Why can't I protect the girl I'm falling for and still keep the Hellhounds out of it? They don't have to be a part of this except to keep an eye on her, that's all. Anything else is on me."

Tony raises an eyebrow. "You're falling for her?"

"I…" There's no point denying it. "I am."

He nods, pulling himself to stand. "It all makes sense now."

"Even if I wasn't, it's the right thing to do, Tony." I search his eyes, trying to convey how important this is to me.

He lets out a slow, drawn-out breath. "I know it is, but it's still a huge risk you're undertaking, and by proxy, the Hellhounds are too." He walks to the door, swinging it open. "I just hope you know what you're doing."

CHAPTER TWENTY-ONE

SAM

The smell of lasagne wafts through the air as I finish cleaning up the dishes and wiping down the bench. Lasagne is, and always will be, a comfort food to me. It reminds me of days spent in my grandmother's kitchen, where she taught me how to read recipes, measure ingredients, and turn the mundane into something delicious. I remember singing to Buddy Holly while carefully layering the meat sauce with pasta sheets, homemade of course, and then spreading the top with oozy cheese sauce. It was my grandfather's favourite, and it quickly became mine too. After every bite, he'd turn to my grandmother with pure joy, and he'd exclaim how exquisite it was. I knew he wasn't just talking about the food.

"You've outdone yourself, sweetie-babes," he'd say. "It is... perfection." And he'd kiss the tips of his fingers.

I always hoped I'd have a love like theirs. One that lasted through the ages. I wanted a husband who'd dance around the living room with me, hold my hand as we strolled through the park on a summer's day, and light a fire to keep me warm at night. A man who cherished me for who I am. An impossible task when I barely know myself anymore.

I've spent too long under the thumb of men who never really cared for me, and now my true identity is unknown even to me. Moving from town to town hasn't given me the opportunity to forge friendships, or any type of relationship, for that matter. I have no hobbies to speak of, unless you count cooking for the man who's taken it upon himself to be my personal protector. It's been so long since I've had any semblance of freedom, and I don't know what to do with myself. I don't know how to find myself anymore.

"Something smells good." Jericho tosses his keys on the table as he closes the door. "Lasagne?"

I turn, resting my hip against the counter and throwing the tea towel I'm holding over my shoulder. "Mmhmm. My grandmother's recipe."

"I meant what I said earlier, you know. You don't have to cook for me." He rounds the counter, his eyes dragging over the length of my body before settling on my face. "Not that I don't appreciate it, of course." He smirks, but there's a wariness in his eyes. "I don't ever turn down a home cooked meal. Better than what I manage to scrape together most nights."

"I know I don't have to, but I want to. I mean, I'm here, so I may as well put myself to good use."

He runs his tongue across his bottom lip. "I can think of plenty of ways to put you to use, princess. And cooking isn't one of them." He chuckles, his lips falling into a smirk. "But I'll take it."

Butterflies swirl in my stomach as I avert my gaze, shuffling my feet. Why does he make me so nervous? He's been nothing but kind to me, and yet, the way his eyes follow me is almost possessive, territorial. And for whatever reason, it doesn't scare me. Quite the opposite in fact.

"I'm doing it again, aren't I?" He cups my jaw, tilting my face up. "Making you nervous."

My eyes search his, but all I see is warmth. "A little," I say, swallowing thickly. "You're rather intimidating, you know."

A crease forms on his brow. "I don't mean to be. Not with you anyway." The corner of his lip curls up in a boyish grin. "I only want you to feel safe here."

"I do." And it's the truth. He might make me feel all kinds of confusing feelings; things I have no right to feel, but of them all, safe is the strongest.

"Good." He ducks his head, pressing his forehead to mine. "I know this can't be easy for you, but it's okay to let your guard down around me. I won't let anyone hurt you."

Easier said than done. "I'm trying." The words are but a whisper.

He brings both hands up to cup my face. "Try harder." His voice is hoarse, gravelly, and it does something to my insides.

His lips brush against mine, the touch fleeting.

I want nothing more than to press myself into him, but I'm terrified at the same time. What if I freak out again?

But what if you don't?

He goes to pull away, but I don't let him. Closing my eyes, I reach my hands up to curl around his neck. My lips find his, and everything else fades into the background. As if I've broken some barrier, his hips press into mine, pinning me against the counter. He slides one hand into my hair, his fingers threading through the strands and gripping. I gasp, pulling back briefly, our breaths mingling in the space between us.

"Are you okay?" Jericho loosens his grip, and panic takes over. I clutch his shoulders, holding him in place.

"I'm fine. Please, don't stop." My cheeks burn as I meet his hooded gaze.

He hesitates, his tongue raking across his bottom lip. "Are you sure?"

No.

Yes.

I don't know.

"We can stop, princess. I don't want to do anything you're not ready for." His hands slip from my hair to my arms and down to my waist, and I lean my forehead into his chest.

"I want this. I do. I'm just… I can't…"

“You need to go slow.”

“I don’t want to…”

“But you need to. I get it. I’m sorry. I forget myself around you.”

Lifting my head, I fist his shirt in my hands. “Please don’t apologise. You’ve done nothing to apologise for. It’s me. I’m broken.”

“You’re not.” His words are growled, as if it hurts him to admit.

A soft laugh escapes my lips. “I am. I have been for a while now. But maybe it’s time I tried to mend myself. I’ve spent so long running from my life, but I don’t want to do that anymore.” I glance around the home Jericho has built. From the worn couches to the prints on the walls, and even the coffee table; it’s minimalist, but it’s his. “I want this. I mean, not *this* exactly, but… a home. A place where I don’t have to look over my shoulder all the time.” I flatten my palm across his chest. “I want to feel something other than fear. And more than anything… I want to feel love and be loved.”

“You can have all of that, princess. Lord knows you deserve it after what you’ve been through.” He tucks his fingers beneath my chin. “But you can’t rush these things. And that’s on me. I shouldn’t keep pushing for something I know you’re not ready for.” I go to speak but he stops me with a gentle kiss. “We’ve got all the time in the world. I’m not going anywhere.”

And I feel it then. A tiny piece of my heart stitching itself back together, the seams pulled tight.

CHAPTER TWENTY-TWO

JERICHO

"All clear. They left five minutes ago." Zeb has been keeping watch over our P lab for the past few weeks now, building up a list of their comings and goings. Every Thursday afternoon she heads out to do her chemist runs, and for around an hour, he disappears in a car with tinted windows.

"You're sure? There's no one home?" I give Matiu the nod, and he swipes the prepared bottle off the bar and unscrews the cap. The smell of petrol fills the air as he stuffs a piece of alcohol-soaked fabric into the top and seals it up again.

"Watched them leave with my own eyes. They're not here."

"Okay, hold tight. We'll be there soon." I end the call, shoving my phone into my pocket and grabbing my jacket. "You ready?"

Matiu nods, holding the bottle in the air. "As I'll ever be." He swipes his lighter from the counter and tosses it into his pocket. "You sure one bottle is enough?"

"How the fuck would I know? I'm not in the habit of committing arson." I stalk down the hall towards the parking lot. By-passing our bikes, I head for the beat-up Holden Commodore we use when we need to be discrete.

"The fuck do you think you two are going?" Stubbs calls out from behind.

I turn to greet him with open arms. "We got the call."

"And you're gonna leave without me? The only one of us who has any experience in this shit?"

I glance at his disfigured hands with a smirk. "I don't know if that counts as experience, Stubbs. You need to actually be good at it." I chuckle, walking backwards, swinging the keys between my fingers.

"That was your father's mistake, not mine," he warns with a gap-toothed grin. "Everything was going to plan until he put his big foot in the way and set the damn thing off early." He shakes his head. "Of course that prick got away without a scratch, and *I* lost the use of half my fucking hands and had to wait weeks for my eyebrows to grow back."

We all know the story, but Stubbs will take any chance he can to remind us how he made it out by the skin of his teeth while everyone else was unharmed. It's his war story, and I don't mind hearing it over and over. Beats thinking about all the ways Jeremiah Lawson fucked up my life for a change.

Climbing into the front seat, I put the key in the ignition and fire it up, pressing the gas to warm her up. She doesn't get taken out as often as she used to, not now that we try to stay under the cops' radar and work on the straight and narrow. We haven't dealt in weapons for years now, and with Tony at the helm instead of my father, the Hellhounds have really turned a corner.

This plan is a step backwards, heading into the grey area of what we're about, but if there's one thing I can't abide, it's methamphetamines. That shit will destroy families quicker than anything else on the planet, and it doesn't discriminate. You could be a high-flying lawyer at the top of your game, but you get a taste of meth and you're just like all the rest of them. Desperate for another hit, willing to do almost anything to get one. You lose friends, family, all sight of what's right and wrong. And before you know it, you're wrapping a noose around your neck and taking a leap you can't come back from.

Stubbs climbs in beside me, and Matiu takes a seat in the rear, the bottle held firmly on his lap. "How close do we need to be for this to work?"

"Depends how good your arm is." Stubbs grins. "I could do it from the car, but you—" he turns in his seat to eye Matiu, "—you might need to walk right on up to the window and throw it from there."

"Pfft, whatever, old timer." Matiu leans back against the seat. "I played league. I know how to throw."

"You ever throw a ball lit on fire?" Stubbs quirks a brow. "Completely different kettle of fish there, boy."

"You kidding me? Every ball I threw was on fire." He flicks his fingers. "Yeow!"

We coast down Boundary Road, past the spot where Sam's car broke down, past her little beach house, and on to a secluded street off to the side. Zeb flashes his headlights from the treeline opposite the house and down a bit. I pull the car up alongside him, and he leans in through the window.

"I reckon we have about twenty minutes tops before he comes back."

I nod. "Good work, kid. You head on back. We'll take it from here."

His face drops. "I can't stay and watch?"

"Not unless you wanna get caught. None of us can. We hit it and run. Best if you're nowhere near here when the shit hits the fan."

"Aww shit, I was looking forward to that part."

"Eh." Stubbs rolls his shoulders, leaning across me. "You've seen one fire, you've seen 'em all. You're not gonna miss anything, kid."

He turns back to me, and when I nod towards his bike, his head drops to his chest and he lopes away. I wait until he's a few hundred metres down the road before swinging the car around and doing a drive-by.

"All set?" I ask as Matiu unscrews the cap once again. He winds his window down and nods, gripping his lighter in one hand, and the bottle in the other.

"Good as." I speed up, pull the car around again, then drive slowly by the house, as close to the fence line as I can get.

The lighter clicks open and the wick catches. He holds the flame to the rag, watching the frayed edges catch, smouldering and wafting smoke through the car. He runs it down the length of the loose fabric, and once the orange flame flickers to life, he drops the lighter to the seat beside him, hangs out the window, and hurls the bottle through the air.

It seems to take minutes, though I know it's merely seconds, before it breaks the glass of the large front window and smashes against the ground. Instantly a ball of flame roars up, igniting the fumes throughout the house. Someone yells, and the door flings open.

"Shit!"

"Go, go, go!" Stubbs yells, yanking on the steering wheel.

"We can't—"

"It's too late! The whole place is gonna go up! We have to get outta here!"

I hesitate, watching as a skinny guy in jean shorts and a singlet stumbles down the steps.

"Go!"

Forcing my eyes back on the road, I gun it, planting boot and racing away from the scene of the crime.

There's a loud boom as we round the corner, and billows of black smoke fill the air behind us. I race to the next corner, taking it too fast and skidding sidewards, but I pull it around and snake down the road until we come to another side street. Slowing the car, I take this turn too, winding our way towards town.

No one says a word, but I know we're all thinking it. *Did he make it out alive?*

CHAPTER TWENTY-THREE

JERICHO

"Explain to me again how this happened?" Tony stands over Zeb. "Because I'm damn sure I told you to make sure no one was inside. No one!" he roars.

"Come on, Tony, he made a mistake. Go easy on him."

Tony swings around to point a finger at me. "Tell that to the kid being airlifted to the hospital in critical condition." He brings his finger and thumb to the bridge of his nose. "Need I remind you, this is not what we're about? The Hellhounds don't harm others, not anymore."

"I'm sorry, Tony." Zeb raises his chin, meeting Tony's eye. "I watched them both leave. I didn't know there was anyone else in there."

"Sorry don't fix it though, does it?"

"Neither does yelling at us," I counter, my jaw clenched. "We know we fucked up. But there's shit all we can do about it."

Stubbs sniffs, folding his arms across his broad chest. "It definitely sent a message. Don't think we'll be seeing any more of them round here."

Tony shoots him a glare. "Don't you start."

"Hey, I'm just sayin', we did what we set out to do. Yeah, it went up shit creek, but it still got the job done, didn't it?"

Tony shakes his head, stalking towards the door. "You better hope he comes out the other side. You don't want that shit on your conscience. I know I don't." He wrenches the door open, then stops, turning to look me square in the eye. "Never again, Jericho, you hear me?"

I nod, knowing full well that it will happen again, only next time it'll be much worse, and it'll be my arse in intensive care, if not six feet under. Dante has the manpower, and without the Hellhounds backing me...

"I'm sorry, Jeri." Zeb's voice wobbles, but he swallows it back, holding his head high.

"It's not your fault, kid. Any one of us could've made the same mistake. Don't beat yourself up about it."

He nods, his shoulders slumped. "Do you think he'll be okay?"

My lips press into a thin line. "I honestly don't know."

He nods again, then turns his head and sniffs. The poor kid. His first real job as a Hellhound and it goes tits up.

Slapping a hand on his shoulder, I give him a squeeze. "It'll be alright, Zeb."

I trudge upstairs, the day weighing heavy on my shoulders. Perhaps my old man was right; I'm not so different to him after all. The first sign of something I don't like, and I go straight for violence. It may not have been aimed at a person, but someone got hurt all the same.

Pushing the door open, I toss my keys on the table and shuck my boots and jacket off.

"Jericho? Is that you?" Sam calls from down the hall, her soft feet padding towards me.

"Yeah, princess, it's me. Sorry if I scared you."

I walk through to the kitchen, pull a beer from the fridge and twist it open, taking a long pull. Placing it on the counter, I brace my hands either side of it, letting my head hang low.

"Is everything okay?" Her softly spoken words and the gentle touch of her hand on my back send a wave of calm through me, and I welcome it.

"It's just been a rough day."

"Anything I can do to help?" Her hand moves in slow circles around the centre of my back, and I can't help but arch into it, tipping my head backwards.

"Not really, but this is nice, what you're doing." I let out a long drawn-out sigh.

She moves to stand behind me, both hands now kneading the flesh. "You're so tense."

A humourless laugh falls from my lips. "You have no idea."

CHAPTER TWENTY-FOUR

SAM

I never thought it possible, but my life has taken on that of a suburban housewife since moving in with Jericho. Each morning I awaken to a note on the kitchen counter after Jericho has left for work. On the days I'm not in the salon, I potter about, tidying things, reading magazines he leaves me, baking. Jericho joins me for lunch every day, and in the evenings, we cook together, clean up, and then settle on the couch to watch trashy TV.

I curl into his side while he rests his hand on my thigh, his thumb rubbing up and down. True to his word, he doesn't push me for anything more than a kiss, and though at times, that can be frustrating, it's what my soul needs to heal. And bit by bit, the broken shards inside me soften and mould into a new me. A whole me.

We've been doing this little dance for three weeks now. He kisses me goodnight, then makes up his bed on the couch, while I lay down in his sizable bed down the hall, staring at the ceiling. Part of me wants to stand in the doorway in one of his t-shirts and beckon him to join me, while the other part of me is still a frightened little lamb. I'm no fool. I know Jericho is not the type of man to be gentle in bed, and while that excites me, it also terrifies me.

Dante was not a gentle man. He took what he wanted, when he wanted, and he didn't give a damn whether I enjoyed myself or not. In fact, I often thought he preferred it if I didn't. Like some sort of power trip. And though I know Jericho would never hurt me, I can't trust that my body won't react differently. The pain of my past is etched firmly in my skin like a brand, and that's not something you forget easily.

Do something every day that scares you. Isn't that what they say? It's that thought running through my mind that has me imagining what it would be like if I were to let go and let Jericho in. Just a little bit. One baby step forward; small enough that it doesn't send me reeling back five feet.

I picture his hands sliding beneath my shirt, lazily dragging up towards my bra. The warmth of his palm as it cups me gently over the lace, his thumb circling my nipple as his lips trail down my throat. A ragged gasp falling from my lips as his tongue finds my nipple and laves circles until it forms a tight bud. My back arching off the bed, his hands gripping my hips…

"Sam?" There's a knock on the door before Jericho eases it open. "Everything okay? I thought I heard something."

I clutch the sheets to my chest as my breath comes out in pants. Jericho frowns, stepping farther into the room. "What is it? What's wrong?" His eyes dart about, searching, but all I can do is stare. Moonlight casts a glow over his bare chest, and I can't help but follow the trail of hair leading from his navel to below his boxer briefs.

"Sam?" The worry in his voice forces me to focus, and I shake my head, pulling myself upright.

"Everything's fine. I'm sorry if I woke you." My cheeks heat as I cast my gaze back over his body, and I pull my bottom lip between my teeth.

Jericho leans his shoulder against the doorframe, his body relaxing as he folds his arms. "You didn't wake me, princess." He rakes a hand through his hair, a smirk gracing his lips. "I had other things on my mind."

I scrunch my eyes closed. "Me too," I whisper.

He straightens. "Yeah?"

I nod. "Could we, um… could we try something?" The words are out before I can stop them, and I swallow nervously. I don't know if this is a good idea or not, but it's out there now. No going back.

"What do you have in mind?" He stretches his arm up to grip the top of the door, as if he has to hold himself back. It doesn't escape me that he hasn't come near the bed, just stayed by the door as if afraid he'll spook me.

"I was wondering if you would… stay… with me. In here." I pat the space beside me. "It can't be comfortable out there, and there's so much room in here… and…" I meet his gaze. "I want you close."

The veins in his arms seem to pop, as if it's taking all his strength to be still. He rocks forward on the balls of his feet. "Are you sure about that, princess? That's a pretty big step."

"I know, and I understand if you don't want to."

Jericho snorts. "Oh, I want to alright." He lets go of the door and steps towards the bed. His long legs move cautiously around to the side, the moonlight behind his back leaving his face in shadow. "Is this okay?" he asks before going any farther.

I swallow the fear rising in my chest as I remind myself it's Jericho standing before me and not Dante. "Yes."

He leans down, tugging the sheets from the mattress. His eyes meet mine as he lowers himself, perching on the side of the bed. "And this?"

"Yes," I whisper.

The bed dips as he swings his legs up, tucking them beneath the blankets. He leaves the rest of the sheets draped around his middle, his muscular chest on display. Not for the first time, I notice the ink swirling from his bicep, across his shoulder, and dipping down behind his back. It's even more beautiful up close.

"Does it mean anything?" I ask, wanting to reach out and touch it, but holding my hands rigid by my side.

He turns to me with a quizzical expression, and I nod towards his tattoo.

"This?" He runs his fingers over the design before settling his hand behind his head. "It's for my family."

"Oh?" It's the first time he's mentioned his family to me.

"Yeah." He flexes his arm. "The base is my mother, where I came from, you know? But the bulk of it, the vines, they're for the club. They're the closest thing I've had to a family for years." He rolls so I can see the rest on his shoulder blade. "And this is a reminder they've always got my back."

"I love that." My eyes dance along the vines, twisting and curling around each other. It's almost manic in design, but one thing remains constant—it never parts ways. The vines may spread out and meander, but they always find their way back to each other. Like a family should.

I want to ask him where his family is now, and why he only mentioned his mother, but I know all too well how difficult the subject of family can be for people, and something tells me his story could be worse than mine. Instead, I lean up onto my elbow, letting my eyes glance across his frame. "Do you have any others?"

"Tattoos?"

I nod, pulling my lips between my teeth.

His stomach muscles tighten as he raises himself to a sitting position, and he turns his back to me. "Just this one. It's part of the initiation. Every member has one." He angles his body to the right, and in the dim light of the room, I can just make out the shape of a three-headed dog with forked tongues, and the words Hellhounds MC. The middle head lines up with his spine, its mouth hung open in a snarl. It gives the impression of something feral, ferocious. Nothing like the Jericho I know.

"Did it hurt?" I reach out, unable to stop myself from trailing the words emblazoned on his back. What makes a person want to scar their body for life with something so grotesque? So hostile?

"Like you wouldn't believe." He chuckles. "Especially the part right down the centre." He shakes his head. "I'm no wuss. I've been in my fair share of fights and I can hold my own, but having that needle ram continuously into my spine almost had me in tears." He twists his head, peering over his shoulder at me. "You breathe a word of that to the boys and my rep will be shot to hell."

Pursing my lips, I pull my fingers across them like a zip. "Your secret is safe with me."

He rolls onto his back, his hand tucked beneath his neck as he stares at the ceiling. "Good. Can't have word getting out the VP of Hellhounds is a pussy. I'll never live it down."

"Somehow, I doubt anyone would believe me even if I did say something." I sneak a glance at him. "Nothing about you is weak."

"We all have our weaknesses, princess. Some of us are just better at hiding them."

CHAPTER TWENTY-FIVE

JERICHO

This woman will be the death of me.

Leaning my head against the cool shower wall, I let the frigid water cascade down my back. It's getting harder to keep from touching her, especially now that we're sharing a bed most nights. She's right there, within arm's reach every night, and I can't do a damn thing about it.

She curls into my side, her thigh thrown across mine, an arm draped over my chest, and her head in the crook of my arm. Content sighs fall from her lips as I wrap my arm around her, pulling her closer, and it takes all my effort to leave it at that.

I wake with a throbbing head each morning, and I have to try and slip out of bed without waking her to take care of it.

Cold showers have become my friend.

Though after last night and her whispered moans against my chest, it's proving a little more difficult to get rid of. No amount of cold water can stop me imagining her making those moans while beneath me, on top of me, hell, any which way.

"Fuck." I picture her dropping to her knees in front of me, her full lips forming the perfect O shape as she takes me into her mouth.

Sliding my lathered hand down to grip my shaft, I pump slowly from base to tip, all the while picturing her mouth in place of my hand. Her crystal-blue eyes staring up at me as she takes me to the back of her throat. Her long blonde hair falling like a curtain around her face. The hum of her moans around my cock as I rock my hips.

I increase the pace, one hand braced against the wall. She swirls her tongue around the tip, her small fingers taking hold at the base and pumping along in time. Her other hand slides down her body, two fingers dipping inside her pussy. She closes her eyes briefly, whimpering as she quickens her pace.

"Jesus," I hiss under my breath, my fingers tightening as my cock thickens and hot ropes of come cover the shower wall and slide down the drain.

Turning to face the spray of the shower, I spin the dial to warm and quickly wash off the evidence of my lack of control.

With a towel draped around my middle, I traipse out to the hall and down to the bedroom. Sam sits on the bed, staring off into the distance, and I'm instantly on edge.

"What is it?" I stalk towards her, dropping to my haunches. "Sam?"

She frowns, giving a small shake of her head. "I don't know. It's probably nothing." She pulls her lips between her teeth, the way she does when she's worried or nervous.

My eyes dart about the room, searching for anything that could have upset her, but find nothing. I take her hand, and it's then it occurs to me I'm naked but for a towel.

Could she have… Did she… hear me?

"Whatever it is, you can tell me." I swallow the lump in my throat, admonishing myself for losing control like that. "Is it… did you…" I let my voice trail off as I turn towards the bathroom, but her eyes remain set on the window.

I follow her gaze, noting the curtains billowing in the wind. And I understand.

"Did you open it?" Her words are whispered, and there's fear in her eyes. I have to remind myself to tread carefully here. I don't want to scare her any more than she already is.

I stand and move to the window. A small slip of paper is wedged in between the hinges. I slide it out while pulling the window closed. The words *you can't hide from me* are scrawled in rushed handwriting, and I quickly crumple it in my hand, coughing to hide the sound. Shifting the curtain slightly to the side, I peer down to the road below. It's clear. Which means the arsehole was inside while I was in the shower getting my rocks off.

Fuck.

If I tell her, she'll run, and then I'll never see her again.

"Sorry, I got warm and forgot to close it before jumping in the shower."

Her shoulders collapse and she drops her head into her hands as her body curls forward. She tucks her legs up into her middle, forming a tight cocoon as she tips to her side and lies across the bed in the foetal position. Her body shakes with tears of relief.

"Hey, you're okay. I'm here. I've got you." I drop to the floor, curling my body over and around hers. "Shhh, you're okay."

"I thought… I thought…" She hiccups, her words catching in her throat. "I was so scared, Jericho."

"Shh, I know." I stroke her hair, keeping her firmly in my arms as I do a more thorough scan of the room. Nothing out of place, no one lurking. It's a scare tactic. He wants her to know he was here. In this room. Watching her sleep. He wants her scared so she'll run away from the only protection she has.

That fucking bastard.

Sam was right. He won't stop until he has what he wants, and he wants to make sure she knows it.

CHAPTER TWENTY-SIX

SAM

"You girls have anything planned for the weekend?" Jen flips the sign to closed and locks the door. She plonks herself down behind the counter, pressing some keys on the till and waits for the day's takings to print.

Barb steps around the pile of hair clippings I'm sweeping, pushing through the saloon-style doors to retrieve her bag. "The boys are having drinks at the garage to celebrate Holden coming home. Can't be going too far from home if they want Jericho to come now that he's a fulltime babysitter." She rolls her eyes, her voice dripping with sarcasm.

"Barb!" Jen frowns, her bracelets jangling as she points a finger in the air. "You know as well as I do that club would do the same if it was you in Sam's shoes.

Matiu may have his problems, but that boy loves you, and he wouldn't let anyone hurt a hair on your pretty little head. So what if you have to change venues for a bit? It's better than the alternative."

"Geez, *Mum,* calm your farm. I was joking." Barb bumps her shoulder into mine. "You knew I was joking, right?"

"Yeah, of course," I say with a little laugh in my voice. *I didn't.* I can never tell when she's serious or having a laugh. Barb's humour is something that takes a lot of getting used to, and even after months of working with her, I still can't figure her out. Some days it seems like she can't stand me, and other days, like right now, it seems as though we could almost be friends.

"See?" She sweeps her arm around my shoulder, her fingers digging in. "We're all good."

"Hmmm." Jen purses her lips as if she wants to say something but doesn't. She turns back to the till, lifting the tiny arms that hold the notes down and counting them into piles.

I finish up with the sweeping then set the broom back into the closet. Barb leans her shoulder against the doorframe, watching me. "You should come, you know. For the drinks."

"Oh, I don't know. It's not really my thing." I dust my hands down my jeans then dig them into my back pockets. "I'll just get in the way."

"Look, it may not be your thing, but it *is* Jericho's scene. And he won't come if you don't."

Shaking my head, I gather my coat from the hook. "I would never stop him from joining in. I'm fine by myself, especially if they're just downstairs. What could happen?"

Barb laughs sardonically. "You really have no idea, do you?"

"What do you mean?" My eyes widen. "Has someone broken in before?"

Barb snorts. "Anyone who so much as tried to do that would need their head read. You don't cross the Hellhounds unless you have a death wish."

A nervous laugh escapes my lips. "You're joking."

"Am I?" She pushes off from the wall, grabbing her cigarettes from her bag and lighting one as she moves to stand by the back door. "All I'm saying is, Jericho is a protector, and right now, you're his—" she waves her hand through the air, "—ward or whatever. He's not going to be able to let loose if he knows you're by yourself."

"What do you mean he's a protector? He's done this before?" Jealousy surges in the pit of my stomach. *Is this just a game to him?*

"He hasn't opened his home to anyone, if that's what you mean, but yeah, in a way. Look, it's not my story to tell. I'm sure he'll tell you in his own time." She sucks on her cigarette, blowing smoke out her nose. "He cares about you. Like a lot." With her cigarette between her fingers, she points at me. "Just give him a night off and come join us for a bit. You never know, you might actually enjoy yourself."

"That better not be cigarette smoke I can smell, Barbara Daphne Parker." The lights in the salon switch off, and Jen's heels clack against the linoleum floor as she marches towards the back.

Barb cringes, holding her cigarette out the door and waving her other hand through the air. "And she wonders why I call her Mum sometimes. Pulling out the full name like that. Geez." She tuts then takes another drag.

The saloon doors swing open, and Jen pushes through, her hands landing on her hips. "Standing in the doorway is not the same as standing outside, chick. You know they'll have my hide if they catch you smoking in here."

Barb wraps her arm around her middle. "It's cold outside. And it's the end of the day. No one's coming to check now, are they?"

Jen folds her arms, cocking her hip to the side. "I was young once too, you know. If I let you do it once, you'll do it again. And before I know it, you'll be smoking in the salon, and I can't have that."

Barb rolls her eyes, throwing her head backwards. "Exaggeration much?" She makes a show of dropping the cigarette to the ground and stamping it out. "Happy now?"

"As a matter of fact, I am." Jen tosses her coat over her shoulder and totters out the door, giving Barb a nudge with her elbow. "You really should quit before your face starts looking like an old leather handbag. Terrible things, they are."

"I don't know, I happen to like leather handbags," Barb says mockingly. "Lots of character."

"You hear that, chicken? She thinks she's a comedian now." Jen chortles as she pulls the door closed and locks it behind her. "Jokes on her though. Those death sticks will make her old before her time. Mark my words, she'll be a wrinkled old prune within the next few years."

"Tell me how you really feel, why don't you?" Barb pulls out a compact mirror and runs her fingers beneath her eyes as she twists and turns to see each side of her face. Once satisfied, she closes the mirror and tosses it back into her bag. "Not a wrinkle in sight."

"Just you wait—" Jen starts to say before the overhead light flickers then blinks out, leaving us standing in the dark carpark, the only light coming from the moon above. "Sod it."

A wrinkle of unease moves up from my feet to my stomach, settling there. *It's just a blown bulb. It's nothing to worry about.*

"Here." Barb fishes her phone from her back pocket and hits the torch app, lighting up the ground before us. We walk Jen to her car and wait until she's started the engine before leaving her.

"You want a ride?" I ask, unlocking my car and climbing in. I peer into the back seat before tossing my bag in the footwell behind me.

Barb flicks through the screen on her phone, her lips pulled to the side before nodding. "Yeah, if that's okay? Matiu and the boys started early so he can't come get me." She mutters under her breath, "Useless prick."

"You need to go home first? Or am I taking you to the garage?"

"Nah, I'll just come straight over with you. Not like he's going to notice if I haven't changed." She leans forward, fiddling with the dial on the radio until a song by P!nk comes on.

She settles into her seat, turning to stare out the window as her fingers tap to the beat on her thighs.

When I park out back of Lawson's Lugs, Barb climbs from her seat and rounds the car, waiting by my door. "You gonna come in?"

Music and laughter carries on the wind, and I have to admit, it does sound like they're having fun. Having my life ripped out from under me, I never really got the chance to go to parties; only the ones Dante dragged me along to as his pet.

The back door swings open, and there, in the light from the hall is the formidable silhouette of Jericho. My cheeks heat and my throat loses all moisture. It seems to be pooling elsewhere.

"Come on." Barb links her arm through mine. "It'll be fun, I promise. Just have one drink. Let him have this time."

My eyes find Jericho once more, and I already know I'm not going to turn her down. If this is what Jericho needs, then I'm going to give it to him.

CHAPTER TWENTY-SEVEN

SAM

"You sure you wanna do this, princess?" Jericho's hand rests on the base of my spine as he leads me through to the bar out back. The walls are a deep mahogany-panelled board adorned with framed pictures of motorcycles and cars. A black and white photo of a staunch-looking man with a handlebar moustache and tattoos along his arms hangs opposite. The gold plaque beneath reads "Benedict Lawson, Hellhounds MC founder. 1935." On the door at the end of the hall is a wooden sign with Hellhounds Motorcycle Club burned in at the top and five lines written beneath.

#1 May your engine never be idle
#2 May your bottle never be empty
#3 May your bed always be warm

#4 May your brothers have your back

#5 May you ride forever more

Behind the door is the sound of raucous laughter and frivolity; a sound I haven't heard too often in my lifetime. The heady aroma of cigarette smoke wafts on the air, and though it holds no good memories for me, I find it intoxicating.

Jericho stops outside the door, his hand on the handle. "Because you know we can just go right on upstairs if you don't."

"No." I bounce on the balls of my feet. "I want to do this. I want to meet your friends."

A smile graces his lips, and the corners of his eyes crinkle. "Alright then." He pushes the door open and steps through to a chorus of "Jericho!"

His hand stays firm on the small of my back as he guides me to a table and pulls out a stool for me. Barb takes a seat across from me, perching on Matiu's lap. One arm wrapped protectively around her, the other tapping the table. He offers a nod. "Sam."

Jericho stands behind me, his hands resting on my shoulders. The warmth of his chest against my back gives a sense of safety, and I lean into his touch. "You already know Matiu and Barb, and this here is Holden. The man of the hour." He gestures to a beefy guy who looks to be in his twenties. There's a dusting of stubble on his chin, and his hair hangs floppy around his face. Unlike Matiu, he seems to be tattoo free, but I know that hidden somewhere on him will be the club patch.

"Holden's been away up north for a bit. Didn't know if we'd see him back here again." Jericho slaps a hand on his shoulder. "Got a good brain on him, this one. Knows everything there is to know about every engine ever built."

Holden holds out his hand, and I take it.

"Nice to meet you. Sam, was it?" He grins, and Jericho's hand squeezes tight on his shoulder.

"She's off limits."

Holden chuckles, leaning back on his stool and holding his hands in the air. "Anyone with eyes can see that, bro." He leans in, speaking behind his hand. "Blink twice if you need help."

Jericho swipes the top of his head playfully, and Holden leaps up, throwing mock punches in the air. They grapple with each other like two brothers. It's a side of Jericho I haven't seen before, but I like it. He's relaxed, at home with these guys. And I can see why he calls them his family.

"So, first time back here, eh?" Matiu grins. "Let me give you the run-down. That picture in the hall? That's Jericho's grandad. He's the one who set this whole thing up." He waves his hand around the room. "Built it from the ground up." He turns, pointing to an older man with more grey than black in his hair and a long beard to match. "That's Antony Dekker. He was best friend to Jericho's dad back in the day. He's the pres."

Antony's dark eyes seem to take everything in as he looks around the room, and when they land on me, a chill runs down my spine.

"Don't mind him. He looks mean, but he's a pussy really." Matiu grins, taking a swig of his drink. "The fella next to him is Stubbs."

"What about Jericho's dad? He's not a Hellhound?"

Barb coughs, clutching her hand to her chest, and Matiu lets out a low whistle. "We don't talk about him round here. He and Jericho…" He cups his hands then pulls them apart as if a bomb exploded. "They don't get along. Tony took over until—" he raises his voice, "—Jericho gets off his arse and takes his place."

Returning from the bar, Jericho places a drink in front of me. "Plenty of time for that. I'm not interested in calling the shots." His hand finds the small of my back. "You're not giving away all our secrets, are you?"

"Wouldn't dream of it, bro."

"Whatever he's told you, it's probably a lie." Jericho chuckles as he takes the seat beside me. His knee presses against mine.

Matiu scoffs. "Like you haven't already spilled your guts to her. You should hear him when he's down here, Sam. Princess this and princess that."

"Oh, *this* is princess?" Holden nudges Jericho. "I was starting to think you'd made her up, mate. The way you talk about her…" He shakes his head before cracking up laughing.

Jericho's hand lands on my thigh. "They're just jealous."

"Hey!" Barb says, holding her hands out to the side. "I'm right here, you know." There's a light in her eyes as she says it, and it's plain to see there's a lot of joking around that happens here. It makes for a nice change.

"Sorry, Barb. I didn't mean anything by it." Jericho winks at her.

"Yeah, yeah."

"Oh, baby, you know I only have eyes for you," Matiu croons, puckering his lips as she feigns disgust.

Barb crinkles her nose. "You're such a suck up."

"And you love it." He waggles his brows suggestively, and Barb leans into him, pressing her lips to his.

Holden looks on with amusement. "You'll have to excuse those two. No idea how to act in front of company." He turns his back to them, leaning his elbow on the table and hooking a thumb over his shoulder. "I know I've been away a while, but have they always been like that?"

Jericho chuckles. "Give it a few more drinks. It gets worse."

Holden's eyes widen before a grin spreads across his face. "Shit. Hard to believe *he*'s got himself an old lady, and you, the fucking recluse of the club has one, and I'm sitting here, the best-looking one of the lot, with my dick in my hands." He shakes his head. "What's the world coming to?"

"Keep it in your pants, mate. We got ladies present." Jericho frowns at Barb in a tongue war with Matiu. "Well, we have *a* lady present." He chuckles as he brings his glass to his lips.

"And what a lady she is." Holden's grin is cheeky and flirtatious, and I can't help but return it. "Sure you wanna slum it with this ugly lug?"

Beside me, Jericho stiffens, his hand on my thigh squeezing. "Off. Limits."

Holden laughs. "Jesus, bro, still as uptight as ever I see. You know I'm not about to steal your woman." He takes a drink, catching my eye and winking. "Not unless she wants me to." He ducks his head, anticipating Jericho's backhand.

"Sam has more taste than that."

Placing my hand on top of Jericho's, I try to change the subject. "So, this Antony—"

"Tony," He interrupts. "No one calls him Antony, not even his mum."

"Oh, right. So, *Tony*, why is he the one in charge when it sounds like it should be you?" I ask, trailing a finger around the rim of my glass.

"I was too young to take over, so he stepped up. I don't see any need to change that just cos I'm older now." He shrugs, raising his glass in Tony's direction. "He's got a good handle on things. And I can focus on the garage."

"And the *club*? What exactly does it do?" I pull my lip between my teeth, almost scared to hear the answer. Have I jumped from the bed of one gangster into the bed of another?

"Keep the streets safe, mainly. A few have tried to run drugs round here over the years, even had some cooking in an old shed just out of town, until it went up in flames." He catches Matiu's eye as he takes a drink. "And we ride, of course."

"So, no guns? No drive-bys? No bust ups?"

"We're no saints. We've all done things we're not proud of, some more than others, but the one thing we try to stick to is no violence, if we can help it. Like I said, we keep the streets of Brookhaven safe." His tone changes, a bitterness lacing through his words. "Sometimes that requires a heavier hand than usual, but for the most part, we keep it above board." He tugs at the leather jacket over his white tee. "We might look like thugs, but we're not. Not unless we have to be, which is hardly ever anymore."

I purse my lips, staring at a wet spot on the table. A life with no violence in it would be nice. If only Dante saw things that way. His day-to-day life is rife with carnage, and he's the one dishing it out. And now I've gone and got the Hellhounds involved, in something that I *know* will end in bloodshed. The questions is, whose blood?

CHAPTER TWENTY-EIGHT

JERICHO

It surprises me how quickly Sam fits in. I never would've dreamed of inviting her down to hang out, but here she is, sipping on a whiskey like she belongs here. And I suppose, in a way, she fits in more than most. She's used to being surrounded by rough-as-guts men, only this lot wouldn't dare lay a finger on her.

"Another drink?" I ask, tilting my glass towards her.

"Mmm, please." She nudges her glass across the table with a grin. Her eyes have taken on that happy glaze you get after a few drinks, and she seems right in her element. "Whiskey is so much better than cheap wine from the supermarket."

I chuckle, grabbing both glasses by the rim. "There's a lot more where that came from." Pushing through the crowd of rowdy drinkers, I make my way to the bar and hold two fingers up. Cassian tilts his head, swiping the whiskey from the shelf and adding two fingers to each glass with a few chunks of ice. He sloshes a splash of ginger ale into one for Sam. He's wearing his "fresh meat" vest and drinking only water so he can drive everyone home at the end of the night. This time last year it was Zeb in the trenches, slowly working his way up the ranks.

I take our drinks and head back to the table, but Tony catches my eye, beckoning me over.

"Jeri." He pats the seat next to him. "Join us." His tone makes it clear it's not a request.

"Just received word. The kid from the lab is gonna pull through."

"Thank Christ for that." To say I'm relieved is an understatement. It's been weighing heavy on my mind for days.

He tilts his glass towards me. "There's something else I wanna discuss." His gaze turns to Sam, and I already know what he's going to say before he says it.

"Look, I know you don't approve—"

He holds up his hands, palms out. "It's not that I don't approve of her. I'm sure she's a great girl. But Matiu told me about your little break-in. You think it's wise bringing her here?"

"If she wasn't here, she'd still be upstairs. It's no different."

"The hell it isn't." He narrows his eyes. "You've gone and introduced her to them. Hell, she's *drinking* with them, for fuck's sake."

"I don't see the problem."

"The problem, son, is that you've made her real to them." He gestures to the table where Sam is laughing at something Holden has said. "They like her. You said they wouldn't be involved, but you know damn well they won't be able to stand down if all hell breaks loose. They'll join the fight right along with you." He massages his temples. "You've made this whole shitstorm ten times worse by bringing her here."

My jaw clenches, and I fight to keep my voice steady. "I'm sorry you see it that way, but I promised I wouldn't lock her away, and I'm not about to go back on that because you don't think I can handle it."

"That's not what I'm saying."

"It is. And I thought by now I would've proved to you that I'm not reckless like Jeremiah. I won't put the Hellhounds in jeopardy, but I also won't keep her prisoner in my home. If I did, I'd be no better than Dante."

"I don't think you're reckless, Jeri. But I think your judgement is clouded on this matter. You're not seeing it for what it is."

"And what is it that I'm not seeing?" I seethe, forcing the words through clenched teeth. "Please enlighten me."

"You really want me to spell it out?"

"Please."

He stands, pointing a finger at my chest. "You're going to bring this whole damn club crashing to the ground. Dante Costello isn't about to let some jumped-up biker steal his wife out from under him without repercussions. And when he comes for you, he will come with everything he has, and it will not end well. For any of us." He drags his finger through the air as he points at each member. "Take a good look at your brothers, Jericho, because one of these days, they won't all be here, and that'll be on you."

"Jesus, why don't you tell me how you really feel?" I snarl.

Tony slams his hand on the table, sloshing his drink. "This isn't a joke, Jeri."

"You don't think I know that? You don't think that's exactly *why* she's moved in with me?" I rise to my full height, standing over him. "You might be okay with leaving her to fend for herself, but I sure as hell am not."

"You're thinking with the wrong head, son."

"That's fucking bullshit! How I feel for Sam has nothing to do with this."

He quirks his brow, stepping closer. "Doesn't it?"

"No. It doesn't." I don't wait for him to say anything else. There's nothing else *to* say. Turning on my heels, I stalk back to the table, sliding Sam's drink to her.

"Everything okay?" she asks, her brow furrowed. Her hand finds my thigh, and it's all I need to calm down.

Taking a breath, I offer a smile. "Everything's fine, princess."

CHAPTER TWENTY-NINE

SAM

After a couple of hours of sitting downstairs and getting to know the men Jericho shares most of his life with, I'm about ready to head home.

Huh.

Home.

Until now, I'd never considered it to be home, but after a few weeks of living with Jericho, I suppose that's what it is now. It certainly feels like a home. A damn sight more than any other 'home' I've had since my father's deal with the devil. The last time I truly felt as if I had a home was when I was a child, innocent and carefree. When I had no idea of the disappointment the world could throw at you, or the devastating hurt you could feel at the hands of someone you thought loved you.

My childhood had been one of fun and laughter, where I was encouraged to go on adventures and learn about the world. It had been a time when joy seemed boundless, and my father's arms were never too far away. A time when I felt safe to be with him, that no matter what happened, my dad would protect me at all costs. How naïve I'd been.

Now, all these years later, trudging up the stairs to Jericho's apartment, I finally feel a semblance of that life I'd thought was long gone. I have a home now, and someone who cares about me. Someone I *know* won't let harm come my way.

I follow him through the door, taking his hand as he moves towards the couch. He turns to me with a quirk of his brow.

"Not tonight," I whisper, giving a gentle tug. Before I can change my mind, I lead him down the hall to his bedroom. My heart hammers in my chest as I stare up at him with my lip between my teeth.

He brushes a loose strand of hair behind my ear, and I close my eyes, leaning into his touch.

"You want some company tonight, princess?" His voice is husky and low, and it sends swarms of butterflies to the pit of my stomach.

Not trusting myself to speak, I push up on my toes, pressing my lips to his as I wrap my arms around his neck. He tastes like whiskey and smells like musk. His hands circle my waist, holding me close, but not close enough.

Over the weeks, we've become more intimate, toying with gentle touches, but never going further than I can handle. Jericho has been cautious to keep things light, never pushing me, never making me feel as if I have no choice. Because with him, it is *always* my decision. And tonight, I'm choosing him.

With shaking fingers, I slowly peel his leather jacket from his arms and toss it on the chair in the corner of the room. Lowering my hands to his waist, I bunch the fabric of his tee between my fingers and lift it over his head, exposing his chest to me. My eyes trail the swirling ink on his shoulder, and this time, I don't stop myself from touching it. My palm skirts over the design wrapping around to cover his shoulder blade. A low moan rumbles through Jericho's chest, and with his thumb and forefinger, he lifts my chin until our lips are a breath away from each other.

He searches my face, and I try to exude confidence. This is what I want.

His palm slides down my neck to the base of my throat, and my breath hitches. His eyes flick to mine. "Is this okay?"

I nod. "Yes."

Slowly, he drags his palm across to the strap of my dress, pushing it aside. Goosebumps form as his fingers glide gently across my skin. He ducks his head to press his lips to the base of my neck, and I arch, giving him access.

His tongue laves across my collarbone, his fingers finding the other strap and tugging it from my shoulder. The loose fabric pools around my waist, exposing me to him.

Stepping back, Jericho casts his gaze across my bare skin, taking in every inch, as if committing it to memory. "You're so fucking beautiful, princess."

I pull my lip between my teeth, reaching for him. He obliges, pressing his hard chest against mine, our bodies melding together. He slides his palm up the back of my neck to rest at the base of my skull, cupping my head as he takes my lips with his once more. This time his kiss is not so gentle. There's an urgency, but at the same time, I can feel him holding back.

I clutch his shoulders, breaking the kiss and arching my back, offering myself to him.

"Sweet Jesus, Sam. You keep doing that, I don't know if I'm gonna be able to stop."

"I don't want you to stop," I whisper.

He drags his lips from my neck, meeting my heated gaze with one of his own. "You sure?"

I nod and slowly reach my hands behind me, to where the dress sits around my waist. I find the zipper and unfasten it, letting the fabric slide to the floor in a heap around my feet.

Jericho's growl rumbles through his chest, and he presses his forehead to mine. "Sam…"

"It's okay. I want this with you. I'm ready." It's not until I say the words out loud that I realise they're true. For the first time in my life I *want* this. I want to give myself over to him. I want *him*.

Without a word, he scoops my legs around his waist, carrying me to the bed and lowering me to my back. He stands back, his chest heaving. "You're sure?"

I rise onto my elbows and nod. "I'm sure."

His hands fall to the button of his jeans, and he undoes it, his gaze never leaving mine. "You change your mind and want me to stop, you say something, okay? I know I said I wouldn't be able to, but I will."

Another piece of my broken heart slots into place, and I find myself grinning up at him. "I won't change my mind."

He leans forward, bracing his hands on either side of me. "You promise me, princess. I will not do this with you unless you promise."

Unbidden, tears prick my eyes. "I promise."

He brushes his lips across my cheeks. "We don't have to do this."

"No." I shake my head, swiping a hand across the wet streaks on my face. "They're happy tears, I promise. I want this. I want you, Jericho. Please." Bringing my hands up to cup his jaw, I bring his lips to mine. "I want to forget the past. Show me how it's meant to be. I want to feel that with you."

His eyes search mine for a moment, but then something seems to click, and he smirks. "Oh, I'll show you how good it can be, princess. I'll make you forget your own damn name if that's what you want."

He lowers his body to the bed beside me, his fingers dancing across my stomach, pebbling the skin. His hand slides farther down, slipping under the thin fabric of my panties. A gasp falls from my lips as he runs slow circles around my clit. My hips move of their own volition, pressing against his hand, urging him on.

I've never felt anything like it before. Dante was only ever interested in himself and what he needed. He *never* touched me like this. I didn't even know it was possible to feel this good.

Jericho shifts lower, his lips brushing against my stomach, below my belly button, my inner thigh. He grips the cotton of my panties and drags them down my legs. His lips once again kiss my inner thigh, his palms gripping my flesh and pulling my leg to rest over his shoulder. He does the same on the other side until I'm lying there, exposed to him.

With one hand flat against my stomach, holding me in place, he licks his lips then lowers his head. The instant his tongue flicks against my clit, I throw my head back, sucking in air. "Oh my god!"

He chuckles, and the vibration sends another wave of pleasure to the pit of my stomach. "You alright, princess?"

"Oh god, yes." I moan, my hands reaching for his head. My fingers rake through his hair, finding purchase as he flattens his tongue and licks from my entrance to my clit. My hips buck, wanting more.

How have I gotten to the age of twenty-four without knowing this feeling? Without knowing sex could be more than just pain?

It's like every last one of my nerve endings is on fire and the only thing that can put it out is Jericho's tongue. I can't control my hips as they grind against his face, seeking release.

And when he slips a finger inside, I'm done for. My back arches, my hands fist in the bedsheets, and Jericho's firm grasp tugs my legs wider. He buries his face between my thighs, his tongue flexing between hard and soft as it grazes my clit in the most excruciatingly intense way.

"I can't... I don't... Oh!" I cry out, my thighs clamping around his face as wave after wave of ecstasy washes over me. He slows his tongue, dragging it in lazy circles as I come down from my high.

"That was... I have no words." I pant, reaching for him.

He smirks. "I told you I'd make you forget."

Chapter Thirty

Jericho

"You did more than make me forget." She grins, leaning up on her elbows as I lay beside her. "I've never…" She pulls her lip between her teeth.

"Never what?"

She's fucking gorgeous in her freshly sated state. Her blonde hair is dishevelled behind her, and her cheeks are flushed with a rosy hue.

Her eyes dart to where she clenches her thighs together.

I quirk my brow. "You've never done that before?" What kind of guys has she been with? Selfish pricks.

She shakes her head. "No… or…" She covers her face with her hands.

"What? You can tell me." I take her hand and tug it away from her face.

She won't look at me, instead focusing on her hand in mine. "I've never… um… done *that.*"

"You've never…" The penny drops. "Oh." I draw the word out. Yup. Selfish pricks. You always make sure the lady has a good time before you get yours. Always.

But that would also mean… "Wait. *Never*? Not even when you're alone?"

"I…" Her face flushes crimson, and she buries her face in the crook of my arm. "No," she squeaks out.

I can't help the smile that forms on my lips. It's egotistical and I feel like a jerk, but fuck if it doesn't feel good that I was her first in that respect.

"No one's ever made you come?"

She shakes her head again.

"Fuck." Something primal thrums through my veins, like a beating of the chest. *I did that for her. She's mine now.*

I tilt her head to face me. "Anything else you've never experienced but want to?"

Her teeth worry her lip again, and this time, I tug it free, running my thumb along her full bottom lip in a caress.

Moving ever so slowly, she slides her hand down my chest. Her small fingers wrap around my still-hard cock. I hiss out a breath but remain still.

"How do I...?" She shifts her hand, sliding it from tip to base and back again. "Like that?" she whispers, and all I can do is nod.

She runs her thumb around the crown as she slides her hand over the top and back down.

"Fuck." My hips jerk, and my head falls back against the bed. "You sure you've never done this before?"

She shakes her head. "Never." With a glint in her eye, she eases her body down the bed. Her tongue darts out, wetting her lips before she takes me in her mouth.

I fist my hands in the sheets to stop them from grabbing her hair and fucking her mouth like I want to.

She alternates between running her tongue up and down the length and swirling it around the tip, to plunging all of me to the back of her throat. It's sexy as hell, but I'm not about to blow my load in her mouth. Not this time anyway.

Gripping her under the arms, I pull her up the bed to lie beside me, my cock falling from her mouth with a pop.

"Did I do it wrong?" she asks with wide eyes, and I can't help but chuckle.

Kissing her firmly, I shake my head. "Baby, there's no way to do that wrong. Everything you did was fucking great. *Too* fucking great. But tonight is about you, not me."

Sliding my hand down her thigh to rest behind her knee, I bring her leg up to hook over my waist. My hand slides between her legs, and I delve two fingers inside. She reacts instantaneously. Her mouth falls open in a gasp as she thrusts her hips in my hand. I roll her onto her back, nestling between her legs. My cock presses against her entrance, but I don't dare go inside. Not yet.

"Please, Jericho," she whimpers. "Please."

Her hips rise up to meet me, and I drop my forehead to rest on hers. "Not yet, princess." I want nothing more than to ride her bare, but I won't do that to her.

Reaching across to the bedside table, I slide the drawer open and pull out a silver packet. I rip it open with my teeth and slide it on before settling myself back between her thighs. "You sure?" I ask again.

"I'm sure." She lifts her hips, and my tip presses inside. We let out simultaneous sighs as I ease in. I begin slowly at first, sliding in and out at a gentle pace before plunging in to the hilt. And when her nails claw at my back, I lose all control.

She throws her head to the side, crying out with every thrust of our hips. "Oh god!" Her fingers dig into my shoulders, my back, my arms, anywhere they can find purchase. She clings to me, her face buried in the crook of my neck, her lips pressed to my skin.

She's close. So close she's whimpering in desperation. I slide my hand between us, finding her clit and squeezing gently. Her arms wrap around my neck, her breath coming out in shallow pants as she throws her head back. "Oh my god, yes!" Her walls pulse around me, milking me until I can take no more.

"Fuck!" I slam into her one last time, my lips crushing hers in a punishing kiss.

As our breathing calms, I roll off her, removing the condom and tossing it in the bin before turning back to her. I pull her into my arms, kissing the top of her head. "Are you okay? I didn't hurt you, did I?"

She nuzzles into my chest, her arms wrapping around my waist. "I'm more than okay." She peeks up at me with a shy grin. "Thank you."

"Believe me, the pleasure is all mine, princess."

CHAPTER THIRTY-ONE

SAM

"Someone's in a good mood this morning. Good weekend, was it, chicken?" Jen grins as she unlocks the back door to the salon and ushers us inside. She switches the lights on as she shrugs her jacket from her shoulders and hangs it on the hook by the door.

I can't hide the smile that creeps across my face, and to be honest, I don't want to. I want to sing from the rooftops at how happy I am right now. After the past few years, I honestly never thought it would be possible, but here I am, building a life for myself, making friends, and falling for someone.

"It was good, yeah." I duck my head, scuttling past her and adding my jacket to the hook.

"It must've been. Jericho was MIA all weekend," Barb quips, a smirk playing on her lips. "Know anything about that, Sam?"

My cheeks redden as I hide my face in my hands. "I might." A girlish giggle erupts, and I shake my head, trying to pull myself together.

"I knew it!" Jen claps her hands and bounces up and down on her heels. How she doesn't break her ankle is beyond me. "Tell me everything. Don't leave anything out." She drags one of the chairs out from the table and sits, her elbows on the table and her chin resting in her hands. "We haven't had any juicy gossip in ages."

"It's hardly gossip if it comes from the source, Jen." Barb rolls her eyes. "And I think I can live without a step-by-step break down of what went down once you got your freak on." She shudders. "I don't need those images in my life."

"Well you can just head on through and get the place set up then, can't you?" Jen waves her away. "*I* want to hear it all." She leans in with a huge grin on her face.

It reminds me of a time when I was younger and I'd sit around the field with my friends at lunchtime, eagerly sharing our secrets and dreams, talking about boys we liked and girls we hated. It was all so frivolous, but it was also what bonded us together. A dull pain twists around my heart at the memory. I never even had the chance to say goodbye.

Jen waves her hand, her bracelets jangling down her forearm. "Don't keep me in suspense."

With a grin, I pull up a chair and angle my body towards hers. "It was magical."

Barb gags. "Eww. What are you? A Disney princess? Pfft. Nothing about those boys is 'magical'."

"I thought you were setting up?" Jen says with a glare then turns back to me. "Carry on."

"I know it sounds corny, but I haven't really…" I wobble my head side-to-side. "You know… *been with* many men. It's never been enjoyable before."

"Aww, honey." Jen reaches over and rubs her hand along my arm. "I'm sorry. Some men can be right jerks when it comes to love."

I cough out a laugh at that. "What Dante and I had wasn't love. It wasn't even like."

Jen's brow creases. "He didn't… *force* himself on you, did he?"

I nod. "Sometimes, yeah. Sometimes I'd just go with it, you know? I'd lie there and let him do his thing. It was easier than fighting him off."

Jen's hand tightens on my arm, and I place my hand over hers. "It's okay. I didn't really know any different." I give a shy smile. "Not until Jericho."

"Aaaand that's my cue to leave." Barb turns on her heels and pushes through to the salon. There's a sound of crunching glass as the light flicks on. "Oh shit."

Jen and I turn as the saloon doors swing shut behind her, and it's then the scent of copper fills my nostrils. We exchange a look before climbing to our feet.

"What on earth is—" Jen stops, and I crash into her. "Oh my god." Her hand flies to her mouth, and I squeeze past to get a look for myself.

Shards of broken glass cover the floor. Every mirror has been smashed, the chairs upended, and on the walls is a smear of something red and sticky, with the words 'time's up' plastered beneath.

My blood turns to ice in my veins as I stare at the carnage. *Time's up.*

It's a message for me. I know it is.

Dante is tired of waiting.

Time's up.

Jen picks her way to the front of the salon, opening the till. "Money's all here."

Barb checks the front door. "Still locked."

"We should call the police," Jen says more to herself than anyone else. She fumbles for the phone and lifts the receiver.

Barb is staring at me, an odd expression on her face. "We should call Jericho."

I shake my head, silently mouthing the word *no*. I don't want him involved. I don't want any of them involved. I couldn't live with myself if they were hurt because of me.

This is my fault. I brought the devil to town, and now I have to make him go away.

Backing out of the room, I blindly search for my jacket and keys as tears fill my vision. He's never going to stop coming for me. I know this. No matter where I go or what I do, he'll always find me, but at least I can draw him away from these people I've come to love.

With a sob wrenching from deep in my heart, I yank the door open and race to my car, ignoring the shouts from behind me. My shaking hands fumble with the keys as I try to unlock it, but somehow I manage. I fling my bag across to the passenger side, pull my door closed and start the engine. It's not until I've backed onto the road and started towards the highway that I look into the rearview mirror and see a set of dark, menacing eyes staring back at me.

It takes all my concentration to keep the car from careening off the road as I stare back at my husband.

"Hello, Samantha."

CHAPTER THIRTY-TWO

JERICHO

"What do you mean she just took off?" Fear and rage course through me as I take in the destruction at A Cut Above. This wasn't a break-in or a robbery, this was a message; one I should've been expecting. I let myself get caught up in what was unfolding between us instead of protecting her like I promised. If he so much as lays a finger on her… My fist connects with the wall, leaving a hole. "Why didn't you stop her?"

"Hey!" Barb glares at me, her hands on her hips. "Calm the fuck down. This isn't our fault."

She's right. It's Dante's fault.

"I'm sorry, Jericho." Jen's voice wobbles as she dabs a tissue beneath her eyes. "We tried to stop her, but she had a head start on us."

"Did she say where she was going?"

"Yeah, between seeing this mess and running out the door, she wrote down her destination." Barb rolls her eyes, folding her arms across her chest. "What do you think?"

"She didn't say anything," Jen offers, her voice almost drowned out by the rumble of a bike pulling into the parking lot.

"Barb!" Matiu storms through the door, sweeping her into his arms. "What happened? Are you okay?" He seems to search her for injury until she waves him off.

"I'm fine, but Sam is missing, and the place has been trashed." She points through the door to the mess of broken glass.

Matiu swings his gaze to meet mine. "Dante?"

"Has to be."

"You think he has her?"

I rake a hand through my hair. The possibilities are endless. "I don't know." I nod at the words scrawled across the wall. "But I'd say it's pretty likely."

"Shiiiiit."

"You can say that again."

He steps away from Barb, running his thumb along his jaw. "What are we gonna do?"

"*We* aren't doing anything."

"Jeri, come on, man. You can't do this on your own." He slaps his hand on my shoulder. "We're all in this together, just say the word."

"I appreciate it, but I can't ask you to do that. It's not your fight." My eyes sweep over the broken mirrors and words written in blood. The only thing holding me together is knowing it's not her blood on the walls. She was with me all weekend.

"Bro, she's your old lady, right? That makes her worth fighting for." Matiu pulls his phone out. "I'll make some calls."

"No." I push his hand away. "You need to stay here with Barb and Jen. I can handle this."

"Bro…"

I level him with a stare. "We don't know that he has her. For all we know, he could still be lurking about. Or that goon of his could be around. Do you want Barb to be here with no protection if he decides to come back?"

"Fuck. No, I don't." Matiu's hands form fists at his sides.

"You need to stay with them. Keep them safe. I'll sort Dante out." *If I can find him.*

Matiu shakes his head. "I don't like this, bro. I know you think you're hot shit, but this isn't some P lab or tinny house you can just run out of town. This is big time."

"Which is exactly why I don't wanna drag the Hellhounds into it."

"Jesus, Jeri, you're not dragging anyone! You're the fucking VP! Where you go, we go. If you've got a fight, so do we. It's how families work, bro. Your shit is our shit."

"Not this time." I stalk towards the door. "You're needed here. You have your own family to protect."

Out in the carpark, I pull my phone from my pocket and call the one person who will understand.

"What's going on?" Tony's gruff voice is oddly calming.

"I need to know where to find Dante."

"Jesus, Jeri, we've been over this."

"Goddamn it, Tony! This is important!" I slam my hand down on the leather seat of my bike before dropping to my haunches. "Please."

There's a rustling sound and muffled voices, then the click of a door. "Talk to me. What's happened?"

"She's gone." My voice breaks, and I hang my head. "Shit went down at A Cut Above, and now she's missing." I pause to get a hold of myself. "I think he's got her, Tony."

"Fuck." There's silence on the other end, and I have to pull the phone from my ear to check we're still connected.

"I can't lose her."

He sighs, and I can tell from the groan of leather, he's just sat down. "I know. And you won't."

"She never said where they lived, and I never thought to ask."

His voice is strained when he replies. "I know where you'll find him."

"Where?"

"He has a section not far from here. There's an old shed down the back of the property, looks like it's been through the eye of a twister and out again."

I frown. "Doesn't sound like the place of a wealthy man. And why would Sam try and hide here if he has a place so close?"

"I doubt she knew it existed."

"How do *you* know it exists then?"

There's a pause, and I can hear his fingers tapping on the desk. "Because I've been there before."

"You what?" My fingers grasp the handlebars of my bike, my knuckles turning white. I've known this man my entire life, and now I find out he has connections with one of the most notorious men in the country?

An image of a distraught Tony showing up on our doorstep late one night flicks into my mind. I must've been about seven at the time, because it was before Jeremiah started using his fists instead of words. I don't recall what was said, but I remember the tension in the room as Tony begged my father for help, and he refused.

"I've been there before, Jeri. I should've told you from the start. I'm sorry."

None of this is making any sense.

"Does this have anything to do with you turning up on our doorstep all those years ago? The night you asked Jeremiah for help?"

There's a sigh, and the sound of his fingers grazing his whiskered chin. "Yeah. It does."

I almost don't want to ask. "Who was it you were looking for that night?"

He swallows audibly. "I was looking for my wife."

Chapter Thirty-Three

Sam

"Did you think you could run from me forever, Samantha?" Dante tuts, resting his forearm on the back of the passenger seat. His hand is cut and bleeding, and I realise it's his blood on the walls at the salon. He didn't send Hannibal to do his dirty work this time, and that thought scares me more than anything. Dante *never* gets his hands dirty.

The blunt barrel of his gun digs into my side. "You've had your fun, but it's time to come home now. No more games. You belong to me."

I sniff back hot tears, determined not to cry in front of him. "I can't give you what you want."

"We just need a little more practise, that's all." He sneers, licking his lips.

A shudder rips down my spine at the thought of him touching me. "No." I shake my head firmly. "It doesn't matter how much 'practise' we have, there will be no heir from my womb." The words sound weak even to my own ears.

That stupid look is wiped off his face, and in its place is one I know all too well. It's the face that haunted my nightmares every night I was on the run. The face of a man with not an ounce of compassion in his blood, only a drive to get what he wants, no matter the cost.

"You underestimate how much I want this."

Something snaps inside. "No. *You* underestimate me. I'll never stop running, and I'll never give you what you want."

His eyes widen, and he tilts his head to the side, as if he can't comprehend what I'm saying. Then he barks out a laugh, slapping his hand on the back of the seat. "I see you've grown some balls while you've been away."

His hand lashes out, grasping my chin tightly between his thumb and fingers. I have to crane my neck to keep watch of the road in front.

"You forget your place."

"How can I forget when you remind me so often?" I spit the words at him.

"And yet you still defy me." His fingers tighten their grip on my face before letting go with a shove. "Obviously you need to be reminded again, and again, and again, until you accept that you have no say in the matter. You will give me what I want, when I want, and if you do not, you will be disposed of, and I'll take your father's debt up with your mother instead."

My brows rise as I stare at him in the rearview mirror. "My mother?" I can't stop the tears from bursting through the banks this time as they cascade down my cheeks. Unbidden, images of my mother's beautiful chestnut hair and eyes of gold flicker through my mind. I haven't thought about her in years, the task too difficult to bear when I was forbidden from seeing her or anyone else from my past. It must have been five years since I last laid eyes on her; her bottom lip quivering as she watched Hannibal escort me from the house.

For a time, I had blamed her for not coming for me. My father had sentenced me to life imprisonment, and my mother had done nothing to stop it. I know now there's nothing she could've done. Dante always gets what he wants, and what he wanted was me.

"She's a little long in the tooth, but I'm sure she can still give me what I want. After all, she bore you."

"You can't!" I cry out, swiping the tears from my face. "I've paid my father's debt—"

"The hell you have!" He jabs the gun harder into my side, making me wince. "He took my son from me. His debt is paid when I get my heir. If you can't provide it, then mummy dearest will."

I close my eyes to his glare. I'd thought my condition was a blessing in disguise; a way to keep him from getting his heart's desire. I thought he'd give up trying. Never in my wildest dreams did I imagine he would turn to my mother to fulfil what I couldn't.

"Turn up here." Dante points to a side street with overgrown weeds along the edge of the road. I slow the car, indicating and checking my mirror. Not a single car in sight.

Dante continues to point out turns along the way, leading me farther from the safety of Brookhaven and Jericho. Had it really only been a few hours since I'd been in his arms? A strangled sob falls from my lips.

"Where are you taking me?" I whisper, all fight diminished. "I thought we were going home."

"That all depends on you, Samantha. You accept your punishment and do as you're told, you'll be rewarded with your old room. Disobey me, and this will be your home for the foreseeable future."

He directs me to another turn, down an even smaller street. "I have a little place out here, in the middle of bum-fuck-nowhere." He grins, his tongue running across his teeth. "It pays to have properties dotted around the country. You never know when one might come in handy. I've had this one for several years, long before you were a twinkle in your daddy's eye." He leers at me, and I lean away, pressing myself against the door. "Haven't had need for this one in, oh, about twenty or so years. Back when someone else owed a debt that went unpaid." He cocks the safety on the gun. "It's up here."

I pull into a long gravel driveway. Dust billows out from under the tyres as I follow the track past two paddocks and onto a packed dirt trail. Up ahead, I can just make out what looks to be an old shearing shed. The corrugated iron is weathered with patches of rust, and the roof has seen better days.

My heart races in my chest. There are no other buildings on the property, and no houses in sight.

This is it.

Either I'm about to meet my maker and have my remains left to rot in the middle of nowhere, or my new prison cell is so far out of the way, even the crows won't hear me scream.

I recognise the black SUV with tinted windows parked by the rickety double doors. Hannibal stands with his hands clasped in front of him, a sneer forming on his lips as I pull up alongside. I don't have to look to know there are others, hiding in the shadows. Dante never goes anywhere without an entourage ready to do his bidding.

"Get out." Dante nudges the gun into my flesh, and I wince. I can already feel a bruise forming.

Hannibal wrenches the door open, taking hold of my elbow. I wave him off. "I can do it."

He glances at Dante before stepping back, giving me room. I unclick the seatbelt and listen as it retracts, stalling for time. Inhaling deeply through my nose, I brace my hands on the steering wheel as I swing my legs around and out the door.

The second my feet hit the ground, Hannibal is by my side, his meaty paw grasping my elbow once again.

Dante stalks past the large double sliders to the smaller door beside them. He pushes the metal frame, and a high-pitched groan ekes out. The sound seems to reverberate through my teeth, and I clench my jaw tight.

Inside, the wooden boards that make up the floor are worn, and in places, missing. Remnants of wool lies in clumps about the vast expanse of open space, and there's an odour that I can only assume is from livestock.

A dingy mattress leans against one wall, a lone chair beside it. Draped over the rafters is a length of chain secured by two large rings attached to the studs running from ceiling to floor. A pair of handcuffs dangles from the chain.

I swallow the lump in my throat. Knowing what I'm up against and seeing it with my own eyes arc two very different things.

"Secure her."

CHAPTER THIRTY-FOUR

JERICHO

"You were married?" I narrow my eyes, thinking back to my childhood, but no recollection of Tony and any woman comes to mind. He was a bachelor through and through.

"I was, but I was an idiot, and I lost her." His voice breaks, and he clears his throat. "Not a day goes by I don't think of her or wish I'd done things differently."

"You got messed up with Dante?" I guess, knowing the answer before he speaks. It's the only one that makes sense.

"In a manner of speaking."

"What's that supposed to mean?" I bark, kicking my leg over the back of my bike. "I don't have time for pussyfooting around, Tony."

He lets out a gruff sigh. "It was your father who made the deal with Dante. He wanted us to run guns for him, among other things. And when he pushed for more… nefarious deals, I didn't like it, and I made it known. I ran my mouth. When one of the runs went bust, Dante blamed me." He inhales a ragged breath. "He didn't bother coming for me, he went straight to where he knew it'd hurt most. Sarah was an angel, and he took her from me. Tied her up… beat and… *raped* her, then left her for dead."

"Oh Jesus, Tony, I'm sorry."

"It took us a few days to find her, and when we did, she was already gone." He's silent, and words escape me. Nothing I say will make this any better.

"You probably don't remember, but I stepped down as VP then. I couldn't face Jeremiah, knowing he was the one who'd brought Dante into our lives. Things went downhill from there, as you know. He started drinking more, got angrier. It was Stubbs who begged me to come back and keep him in line. Fat lot of good that did."

I hang my head, my voice low. "It did good for me."

He sighs. "Yeah, I guess it did. Still didn't stop you getting caught up with Dante Costello though, did it?" There's a jangle of keys down the line. "Listen, I don't want the same thing to happen to Sam as happened to my Sarah. We need to move if we have any chance of getting to her before he…" His voice trails off. He doesn't need to say any more.

"You don't have to come, Tony. I told you I'd do this on my own and keep the Hellhounds out of it. I just need an address."

A door slams and a whistle rings out. "Boy, there is no way in hell I'm letting you walk into the lion's den on your own. I vowed to do right by you, and by Jesus I plan on doing it until my dying day. You best believe I'm coming."

The back door to A Cut Above swings open, and Matiu strides out with Barb on his tail. "Good, you haven't left yet."

I pull the phone from my ear. "What's going on?"

"We're coming with you."

"The fuck you are."

"Sorry." He holds his hand to his ear, squinting his eyes. "I can't hear you." His helmet is in his hands and on his head before I can stop him. "Where we headed?"

Barb swings her leg over the back of his bike, holding onto his waist. She gives me a thumbs up, and I shake my head. Once they get an idea in their heads, there's no stopping them.

I point at Barb. "You will stay outside and out of the way. I'm not having you taken too."

She holds two fingers to her forehead and flicks them out in a salute. "You got it, boss."

"Jeri?" Tony's voice calls faintly, and I lift the phone to my ear.

"Where to?"

"Meet me on Main Street, near the old sawmill. I'll show you the way from there."

"You sure about this, Tony? It's not too late to back out."

"Ain't no way I'm backing out, son. I lost Sarah and Jeremiah, I'm not about to lose you too."

CHAPTER THIRTY-FIVE

SAM

With my hands bound by chains behind my back and secured to the wall, I stare at Dante expectantly. Even on my knees I can barely move without the cuffs cutting into my wrists.

The wooden chair has been dragged ten feet in front of me, and Hannibal is perched there, keeping watch while Dante slowly walks back and forth.

The mattress I'm kneeling on smells dank and mouldy, and there are dark stains through the centre. I don't want to think about what caused them. I don't want to think about anything other than how to get out of this. I'm stranded in the middle of nowhere. There's no way Jericho will be able to find me, and I wouldn't want him to anyway. I never should've let myself get so carried away. It was stupid to think I could be free and have a life of my own. Four years with Dante should've taught me that.

"What are you going to do to me?" I don't know why I ask, except that not knowing somehow seems worse.

He smirks, his fingers steepled at his chin as if deep in thought, but I know he's only toying with me. Stretching it out to make it even more unbearable.

Adjusting my knees, I shift closer to the wall, loosening the chain's pull. I squeeze my fingers together, trying to make my hand as small as possible, then gently tug on my binding. Without some form of lubrication, it won't work though. They're much too tight.

Dante strides back across the room, this time closer to the mattress. He stops in front of me, and I jut my chin out in defiance.

He grins, rolling up his shirt sleeves. "You were never this feisty at home, Samantha. I like it." He draws his hand back and brings it down across my face in a swift motion. The sound reverberates off the walls as I struggle to hold myself upright.

My cheek flames, and blood trickles from my nose into my mouth.

"*That* is for running away." His perfect hair hangs limp across his forehead. He sniffs, jerking his chin and signalling for Hannibal to join him.

I turn my gaze to my surrogate son, willing him to show me mercy, but I know it's pointless. He'll do what Dante asks without question.

He nods, and Hannibal bends his head to the left then right, his bones cracking loudly. His hand swings back and lands on the other cheek with a resounding crack.

My head feels heavy on my neck, and I hang forward, my arms stretched taut behind me. My shoulders scream at me, but I can't pull myself up. Lights dance before my eyes, and blood drips from my nose, creating another patch on the mattress.

Dante sits on his haunches. "Now, Samantha, this hurts me as much as it hurts you." *I doubt it.* "But you have to be taught a lesson. No one runs out on Dante Costello. *No one.*"

Something crashes into the side of my head, and a high-pitched ringing assaults my ears. I swing sideways, almost lying on the mattress, but not quite, the chain keeping me hanging aloft. The angle has my stomach doing somersaults, my mouth filling with saliva. One of my eyes has gone fuzzy, and I can feel it swelling.

There's a muffled voice, but I can't hear over the ringing in my ear. Two hands grab my shoulders and lift me, leaning my back against the stud, the chain digging into my flesh. I try to lift my head, but it is too heavy. I just want to close my eyes and go to sleep.

Thudding. Footsteps maybe? And then cold water is thrown in my face, and I gasp for breath, choking as I inhale droplets.

Clicking fingers dance in front of my face, and Dante leans in close, his hand gripping my hair and yanking my head back. His lips press against my good ear as he whispers, "Don't go to sleep, Samantha. I'm not done with you yet."

CHAPTER THIRTY-SIX

JERICHO

We pull down a small gravel road that seems to lead to nowhere, and Tony climbs from his bike. "We walk from here. If we have any shot at coming out of this alive, we don't want them knowing we're coming."

"You sure you want her coming along?" I ask Matiu as Barb steps from the bike and tucks her helmet behind his.

"Excuse me?" Barb folds her arms across her chest, her hip jutting out to the side. "Who said it's up to him? She's my friend too."

Matiu shrugs, giving me a look that says, *what am I gonna do?* And for once, I don't have an answer for him.

"This isn't a place for women." Tony steps in. "Believe me, you don't wanna be a part of this."

"Well I'm sure as hell not gonna sit on my arse out here all by myself either." Her eyes are narrowed, and there's a fierceness in them. "I'm coming with you."

"Don't say I didn't warn you." Tony shakes his head, muttering about stubborn women as he makes his way through the trees.

"Please, just stay out of the way, okay? We can't be watching you and Sam at the same time, right?" I turn to her with a pleading look, and she lets out a long-suffering sigh.

"I said I would, didn't I?"

Up ahead, Tony signals for us to spread out. Matiu and Barb take the left, and I head to the right with Stubbs, while Tony takes the middle.

If what Sam told me about Dante is correct, he won't be here alone. You can bet his right-hand man will be hanging about somewhere, and I'd be surprised if there weren't others.

Tony holds his hand up, turning to us and pointing two fingers at his eyes then out to the treeline northeast of us. I can just make out the figure of a man amongst the brambles. He hasn't spotted us. Yet.

Crouching low, I keep careful watch of my feet as we push on through. If there's one guard, there'll be more, and I can't risk us being seen before we get to Sam.

Ahead, the shadow of a large barn or shed looms, and I spy two more armed men keeping watch.

We're close.

My heart seems to collide with my lungs as it pounds heavily in my chest. There's no sound coming from the building, but I don't allow myself to think about what that could mean.

Tony points to the right where two large sliding doors hang, and beside it, another smaller door. He gestures for Stubbs and I to move that way then signals to Matiu and Barb to follow him around the back.

"He won't want to go in there. Too many memories," Stubbs offers, nodding at the doors. "We found Sarah just inside." He stops me with a hand on my shoulder. "You need to be prepared, Jeri."

I shake my head, dismissing his words.

"I mean it, son. It wasn't pretty."

"All the more reason to get in there then. We still might have time."

Stubbs gives me a pitying look, but I brush it away. The guard nearest the door has turned in our direction, and I drag Stubbs to the ground with a finger to my lips.

We stay that way a few minutes, watching through the swaying gaps in the trees. Whatever he thought he heard, he can no longer hear it, and the guard swings back to his post.

"I'll take him out. You get to your old lady." Stubbs is up and running low to the ground before I can stop him. All I can do is watch as the guard lays eyes on him, and raises his gun.

CHAPTER THIRTY-SEVEN

SAM

Hannibal loosens the chain, lowering me to the mattress. I roll to my side, blinking up at my tormentors with my one good eye.

Dante leans into my face, tearing the fabric from my chest, leaving me exposed. Hannibal averts his eyes.

"Did you think I wouldn't know what you were up to?" Dante seethes above me, his face contorted into one of pure rage. "Shacked up with one of those *mutts*?" He practically spits the word. "And you let him *touch* you."

I try to frown, but my face won't cooperate. How the hell does he know what I did with Jericho?

"You think you could get away with disrespecting me like that, Samantha?" His voice rises in a way I've never heard before. He's been angry at me, but not like this. Even when he's been dishing out punishments to his lackies, I've never heard such vitriol, and I know I'm not making it out of here alive.

"I let you have your taste of freedom, but I draw the line at sharing you with a filthy mutt." He spits, and it lands on the mattress beside my face.

His fingers dig into the flesh of my waist as he wrestles with the button of my jeans. I could fight, kick out with my legs and make it difficult, but what good would that do? He'd still overpower me, and then he'd go after my mother instead.

A whimper falls from my lips, my breath hitched as I close my eyes, ready to succumb and let him have what he wants.

With a roar, he rips the denim from my legs and tosses it aside. Tears stream down my face as I look to Hannibal, trying to catch his eye. But it's no good. He won't look at me.

Dante lifts my hips, laying them flat on the mattress and spreading my legs so wide it sends sharp pains down my inner thighs. He unbuckles his pants with one hand while the other grabs hold of my breast, squeezing until I cry out. Another sob wracks my body, and I'm silenced with the back of his hand.

"Shut up! You brought this on yourself, Samantha."

There's some sort of commotion at the end of the shed. Hannibal stalks angrily towards the door, and Dante curses, pulling his pants back up. "Don't move."

"Sorry, boss. I caught this one sneaking around back." Someone is thrown forward, landing on their hands and knees, but I can't tell who. They're too far away.

"Antony Dekker, as I live and breathe." Dante lifts Tony's head by the scruff of his hair. "Didn't expect to see you back here."

"I couldn't let you hurt another innocent woman."

Another one? My mind is fuzzy. Nothing is making sense. There was no other woman.

"Couldn't *let* me?" Dante barks out a laugh. "As if you could stop me." He makes a show of looking around. "Looks to me like you're outnumbered."

There's a loud noise like a shotgun blast, and Hannibal takes off out the door. I hear yelling, and Dante backs towards me. "Tie him up. We'll deal with him later."

Another shot. Someone screams. More yelling.

I try to sit up, pulling against my restraints to help me.

"I told you not to move." Dante's boot moves in slow motion as it connects with my jaw. Stars dance in my vision as I tip backwards, the chain wrenching against my arms. Blood fills my mouth, and something else too. A tooth? I spit, but I'm on my back and it falls onto my face, dripping down my cheek and into my ear.

"Sam!"

Jericho? Am I dreaming? Or maybe dying?

Footsteps thunder. A scuffle.

"Do it!"

A loud blast, and another, this time inside. Pain rips through my side, and both ears seem to vibrate as if a bell is ringing inside them. I close my eyes, letting darkness take me.

CHAPTER THIRTY-EIGHT

JERICHO

When Stubbs goes down, I run, tackling the shooter before he can take another shot. His nose crunches beneath my fist as it smashes over and over into his face until he is just a mess of blood and tissue.

"Jeri!" Stubbs calls out, and I turn to see Hannibal crashing towards me. I don't wait for him to catch up, instead taking the opportunity to run for the doors. The element of surprise is gone, and now all I can think about is getting to Sam before it's too late.

I take off, pumping my arms and legs as hard as I can. Hannibal switches trajectory and comes right at me, but I shoulder charge him, sending him off balance.

I'm mere feet away from the doors when I hear another gunshot, and Barb screams. I jolt to a stop, torn between going to my brother and going to Sam.

Dante's voice makes the decision for me, and I charge through the door like a bull through a matador's cape. It takes a second for my eyes to adjust to the dull light inside, but when they do, I see Tony trussed up to the wall, his face a bloodied mess, and on a mattress, stripped to her underwear, is Sam. Dante's foot is raised, and it slams into Sam's face, sending her reeling backwards.

"Sam!"

A rage like I've never known before rushes through me, and I run at Dante. We hit the floor, our bodies a mess of thrashing limbs. He gets the first punch in, square in the jaw, but he won't get another. I have twenty years on the arsehole, and I won't let him have the upper hand.

Wrapping my legs around his waist, I flip us around, my hands pinning his down. Tipping my head back, I bring it down, hard, smashing it into his nose. Blood splatters across his face.

"Do it!" he spits out, and my concentration is momentarily broken.

I turn in time to see one of his men holding a gun to Tony's head. He pulls the trigger, and two things happen simultaneously.

Blood explodes from Tony's head as it lolls against his chest, and Hannibal bursts through the door, his gun cocked and aimed at me. He fires off three shots as he runs towards me, but I roll, taking Dante with me. His body jolts as he's hit. His eyes widen and a wheezy gasp splutters from his lips before he sags against me.

Bang, bang, bang, click.

I heave Dante off me, tossing his body aside like a ragdoll as I stare down Hannibal. He pulls up short, his eyes dancing between the spent body of his boss and the gun in his hand. He frowns, letting it fall to the floor with a clatter.

When he makes no move, I spin around and crawl the short distance to Sam's body. There's so much blood surrounding her, and she's not moving.

"Sam?" I stroke her hair from her face, my fingers sliding down to her throat. I close my eyes, focusing on the weak, thready pulse. She's alive, but only just.

Her face is almost unrecognisable. Her nose is broken, her eye puffy, and her jaw hangs on an odd angle. Blood is smeared from her ear and nose across her face. But it's the blood pooling beneath her that has me worried.

I rip my jacket off and pull my t-shirt from my chest to staunch the blood. As I press down, she moans, and I hush her. "It's gonna be okay, Sam. You're gonna be okay." Lifting her shirt, I find the bullet hole to her side. "Fuck." There's too much blood.

I search my pocket for my phone, but it's not there. "Fuck!"

"Is-is she okay?"

I turn to see Hannibal standing behind me, his brow creased and his eyes set firmly on the pool of blood.

"What the fuck do you think?" I rake my hand through my hair. "She's bleeding out."

He drops to his knees, and I ready myself for a fight.

"Shit." His voice is barely a whisper. "It wasn't meant to be like this."

"What the fuck did you think was going to happen?" I demand.

His eyes fill with tears, and he stares at her with a haunted expression. "She wasn't meant to die." He takes her hand, and it takes everything in me not to swat him away. Perhaps Sam had been right about him having a soft spot for her.

"She doesn't have to die. Do you have a phone? She needs an ambulance."

He swivels his head, blinking at me for a second before reaching into his pocket and pulling out a flip phone.

While he dials, I keep talking to Sam. "Hang in there, princess. Help is on the way. We got you."

"Jeri?" Stubbs voice is strained, but I'm damn glad to hear it. In all the commotion, I hadn't had time to check on him.

"Over here." I twist around, careful to keep my hand steady on Sam's wound. "She's hurt bad, but she's okay." I allow my eyes to flick towards the still body of my friend and father figure. "Tony…" I can't say the words, the wound still too fresh.

Stubbs follows my gaze. His whole body seems to droop with the weight of our loss. The Hellhounds won't be the same without Tony at the helm.

He hobbles closer to our fallen member, dropping to his knees and burying his face in his hands. I can't allow myself to think about it right now. I'll grieve when I know Sam is okay.

Turning back to her, I continue sweeping her matted hair from her face and whispering in her ear. "Come on, princess. Stay with me."

CHAPTER THIRTY-NINE

JERICHO

"You ready for this, bro?" Matiu slaps his good hand on my shoulder. His other is bound in white bandages and slung across his chest. While wrestling with one of Dante's henchmen, the gun had gone off and ripped a hole right through the centre of his hand. The way Matiu tells it, Barb had come screaming out of the trees when the gun went off. She held a log aloft and thwacked the guy around the head with it. He dropped like a fly.

Now there's a diamond-encrusted band on her ring finger, and he's sworn to never leave her side again.

"Can you ever be ready for something like this?" I slip my arms into Tony's vest before donning my jacket.

We head out to the bar where the girls are waiting. Sam is still sporting two black eyes and her jaw has stitches where they had to reset it, but she's never looked more beautiful to me.

In black leggings and a long-sleeved white tee underneath my old vest, she fits right in. She holds her arms out to me, and I step into her embrace, inhaling the fruity scent of her shampoo.

Saying goodbye is never an easy thing, least of all when it's the man who raised you. Tony may have made his mistakes over the years, but he'd always remained a strong presence in my life, and for that I am thankful. Without his guiding hand, I don't know where I would've ended up.

Stubbs tosses the keys my way then hobbles towards the car on his crutches. We trail behind in a sombre line, squeezing into the Holden Commodore.

The roads are quiet, as if they too are in mourning. Grey clouds cover the sky, and there's a hint of rain in the air.

We pull up outside the cemetery, and already a small crowd has gathered around the plot. Stubbs had made all the arrangements, ensuring Tony be buried alongside Sarah so they could be together once more. From what I'm told, Tony never even contemplated the idea of another relationship once she was gone, because 'a love like that doesn't strike twice.'

Sam takes my hand as we walk towards the gravesite, and I know Tony is right.

The procession follows us back to Lawson's Lugs where I had Cassian organise food and drinks. He's playing bar wench again, but this time Zeb is behind the bar with him. He's pouring a round of Jack on the rocks in honour of Tony, and everyone who drinks must salute the legend whose image is perched at the end of the bar.

Sam and I each take a glass, but I can tell she's becoming weary. It's been a long few days, and her recovery hasn't been easy. She should still be in hospital, but she insisted on being here for this.

We make a toast to Tony and tip our drinks back, then I take her hand and lead her upstairs. The celebration of his life will go on into the early hours of the morning, and I won't be missed for an hour or so.

Sam toes off her shoes as soon as we step through the door. She lets out a long, drawn-out sigh. "You okay?" she asks, wrapping her arms around my neck. It's been less than a week since Dante's demise, but already I can see a change in her. A confidence she didn't have before.

I wrap my arms around her waist and plant a gentle kiss to her lips. "As good as I can be." I nod towards her bandaged side. "How about you?"

"A little sore, but I'll live."

Thank fucking Christ for that.

"You want me to run you a bath?"

She quirks a brow, a smile playing across her lips. "I'm perfectly capable of running my own bath, Mr. President. You should be down there with your family."

I grip her hips, pulling her into my body. "You're my family."

"And we've got our whole lives to be together. You only get one send off, and Tony deserves a good one."

"He'll get one, trust me. Come 3AM you'll be begging them to keep the noise down." I rest my forehead against hers. "They won't even know I'm gone for at least a half-hour."

She chuckles, throwing a smirk my way as she turns on her heels and makes her way down the hall. "Half an hour?" She peels my vest from her shoulders and tosses it on the ground behind her. "I think we can fill that in easily." When she reaches the door, she peeks over her shoulder. "You coming?"

You bet your arse I am.

Within seconds I stand before her, my fingers resting on the hem of her tee. "You sure about this, princess? I don't want to hurt you."

She reaches her hand up to cup my jaw, and I lean into it, kissing her palm. "You won't hurt me. I trust you." Her thumb brushes against my lip. "Erase his touch. Make me forget again."

There's no way I can refuse her.

With a gentleness I didn't know I had in me, I ease her top over her bandaged side and discard it on the floor. Her bare breasts fall into my hands, my fingers rolling her nipples until they form tight buds. She lets out a content sigh, her head dropping back.

Lowering my lips to her throat, I kiss a trail up her neck to her ear. She shudders, and a giggle escapes her as my breath tickles the sensitive spot below her ear.

I drag my tongue back down her throat to her breasts, taking each one in my mouth before traversing farther down to her belly. On my knees, I take hold of her pants and slide them from her legs, then do the same with her panties.

My tongue goes back to her belly, drawing lazy circles as I drift lower still. Her breath hitches as I find her inner thigh with the tips of my fingers, then my lips. I guide her to sit on the edge of the bed and lie her back, her legs spread before me like a beautiful smorgasbord. It's a sight I'll never tire of.

With the flat of my tongue, I lap at her opening, flicking against her clit and making her hips jolt. Slipping two fingers inside, I can already feel how wet she is. I can't help but groan as I watch my glistening fingers slide in and out of her, tormenting her slowly.

"Oh God," she croons, and her hips begin to rock.

I flatten my palm across her stomach. "No moving. You'll pop your stitches."

She bites her lower lip but obeys, her hand finding purchase in the bedsheet beside her.

My tongue circles her clit, and I pick up the pace with my fingers, thrusting in and out. I add another, curling it up to find the rough ridge that drives her wild with every stroke.

"Oh fuck!" she cries, and her other hand slams against the bed. Sweat shimmers on her brow as she tries desperately to remain still, but her hips keep moving of their own accord.

She whimpers as I hold her down, my tongue flicking and swirling until I feel her walls clamp down around my fingers and her thighs pull tight around my head.

"Fuck!"

I hold her legs in place, my tongue buried inside her while she rides out her ecstasy.

When her legs begin to shake, I ease up, pulling back and wiping my face with the back of my hand. Her body sags into the bed, sated.

"That was…" She pants, searching for the word but coming up empty, and I can't help but grin.

"You can thank me later." Adjusting my cock inside my pants, I stand, my eyes sweeping across her bandages. "Shit, you're bleeding."

"I am?" She attempts to lift her head, but exhaustion is already claiming her. "It's okay. I'm okay." She flops back onto the bed, curling onto her side.

Padding to the bathroom, I grab a damp towel and some fresh bandages. I dab gently at her flushed skin and change the bandages while she drifts off to sleep, pulling the blanket up to cover her, then I kiss her head and close the door behind me.

Back downstairs, the party is in full swing.

"Jericho!" Holden hollers, beckoning me to join him. "So, you're the new pres, huh?"

I hold my hands out to my sides. "Looks that way, yeah."

"Who's your VP gonna be?" He stands taller, jutting his chest out.

"Fuck off, prick. You've been back on the scene all of five seconds. If anyone is VP, it's me." Matiu tosses his drink back and slams it on the table. "Right, old man?" He gives me a cocky grin, and I can't help but laugh.

"You're dreaming if either of you think you're getting in over me." Stubbs steps forward, waving his crutch in the air. "I've lost fingers to his old man and taken a bullet in the leg for Jeri. I'm the fucking VP."

I cock my head, grabbing a drink from the bar. "He's got ya there, boys."

Matiu flaps his arm in the air. "Ah, hello. I took a bullet too, bro."

Slamming my hand down onto his shoulder, I agree. "You did, and I appreciate it. But it's still going to be Stubbs. It's what Tony would've wanted."

"Well fuck. I can't argue with that."

Zeb pours us all another glass, and we raise it towards Tony. "To our fearless leader, may he rest in peace."

"And to our new leader, finally taking his rightful place," Stubbs says, tipping his glass at me.

"To the Hellhounds. May we ride forever more."

A NOTE FROM THE AUTHOR

Thank you so much for taking the time to read *Cut Loose*. I was asked to take part in a charity anthology called Hellhounds, and this story popped into my head. It's my first romantic suspense/MC romance story, and it won't be the last! There is more to come from the Hellhounds!

Hopefully you enjoyed reading it as much as I enjoyed writing it. If you did, I would love it if you could leave a review. Reviews not only help our work to be seen, they also offer valuable feedback.

Once again, thank you for reading!

Stacey xxx

ACKNOWLEDGEMENTS

Well, here we are, at the end of another story, and the beginning of a new series. I've had so much fun writing this one, mainly because it's not the type of story I normally write and it challenged me.

I need to thank Lasairona for inviting me to take part in the Hellhounds Anthology, without which, this story would not have come to fruition. There's nothing like a wordcount limit and deadline to stir up the inspirational juices.

I also have to thank Trina, as always, for letting me bore you with updates on my story and the constant nit-picking I do at the editing stage. Thank you also for going through my words with a fine-tooth comb and making sure everything is as it should be. I appreciate everything you do!

Nicole, for being my cover guru and someone I can bounce ideas off. You keep me motivated and always see what I can't when it comes to covers!

And last, but certainly not least, I have to thank each and every reader who takes a chance on my books. I still can't quite believe there are people all over the world reading what I write. It blows my mind.

About the Author

Stacey resides in Ashburton, New Zealand with her husband and three children. She is a qualified proofreader, author, wife, mother, and self-proclaimed culinary goddess. When she's not busy writing or editing books, she enjoys reading and procrastinating on TikTok.

She absolutely loves hearing from readers, so please feel free to reach out via email, Instagram, or join her reader group, Broadbent's Bookish Babes.

www.staceybroadbent.com

OTHER BOOKS BY STACEY BROADBENT

Standalone
Never Judge a Book
Emma
Deep Heat
Lady Luck: A Deep Heat bonus novella
Fever

A Step in Time series
Dancing through the Storm
Dancing in Circles
Dancing with Destiny
A Step in Time: the complete series

Super Mum series
Frazzled
Frazzled and Frumpy
Frazzled, Frumpy and Fabulous!
Super Mum: the complete series

Dark sins novellas
Sins of the Flesh
Mine

Short Stories and Poetry
Musings, Mournings, and Misadventures
Musings, Mayhem, and Mystery

Anthologies
Scars to your Beautiful
Witching Hour: Vices and Virtues
The White Ribbon Collection
Key to my Heart
A Touch of Inspiration
No Place Like Home
Serendipity
Lucky Star
Hellhounds